Her *warmth,* her *curves,* awakened him.

It would have been so easy to just give in and carry her to the floor, but he remembered her vulnerability.

Just as he would have released her, she lifted her head, and her lips found his. Her kiss was the brush of a butterfly wing, so light he barely felt it, but it sent an electric jolt to the farthest cells of his body.

He almost swore. She deserved so much better….

As the thought formed, she moved against him, just a little, a soft murmur escaping her as she sought a deeper touch from his mouth.

He couldn't resist. No way. He needed this kiss more than anything in his life. He lowered his head, pressing his mouth to hers, gently at first, then more deeply as she welcomed him.

"Ethan…"

His name sounded like a prayer as she whispered it. Buried parts of his being burst free of their bonds, reminding him he was a living, breathing man.

It would have been less painful to rip off his own skin, but he pulled away, conscience piercing him like a dagger.

She looked at him from sleepy, worried eyes. "Ethan?"

"I don't want to hurt you. I'm afraid I might. I can't even trust myself, Connie. How can I ask anyone else to trust me?"

ROMANCE

Dear Reader,

Be sure to add Silhouette Romantic Suspense's July offerings to your summer reading. Especially since *New York Times* bestselling author Rachel Lee is back in the line! And she's continuing her wildly popular CONARD COUNTY miniseries with *A Soldier's Homecoming* (#1519). Here, a hunky hero searches for his long-lost father and unexpectedly falls in love with a single mom whose past comes back to haunt her. You'll need to fan the flames for Sheri WhiteFeather's sexy romance, *Killer Passion* (#1520), the second book of a thrilling trilogy, SEDUCTION SUMMER. In this series, a serial killer is murdering amorous couples on the beach and no lover is safe. Don't miss this sizzling roller coaster ride! Stay tuned in August for Cindy Dees's heart-thumping contribution, *Killer Affair*.

A snowstorm, a handsome bodyguard, an adorable baby and a woman on the run. You'll find these page-turning ingredients in Carla Cassidy's *Snowbound with the Bodyguard* (#1521), the next book in her WILD WEST BODYGUARDS miniseries. In Beth Cornelison's *Duty To Protect* (#1522), a firefighter comes to the rescue of a caring crisis counselor as she wards off a dangerous threat. Their chemistry makes for an unforgettable story.

This month is all about finding love against the odds and those adventures lurking around every corner. So as you lounge on the beach or in your favorite chair, lose yourself in one of these gems from Silhouette Romantic Suspense!

Sincerely,

Patience Smith
Senior Editor

RACHEL LEE

A Soldier's Homecoming

Silhouette®
Romantic
SUSPENSE

 SILHOUETTE BOOKS

ISBN-13: 978-0-373-27589-2
ISBN-10: 0-373-27589-7

A SOLDIER'S HOMECOMING

Visit Silhouette Books at www.eHarlequin.com

Printed in U.S.A.

RACHEL LEE

was hooked on writing by the age of twelve, and practiced her craft as she moved from place to place all over the United States. She now resides in Florida and has the joy of writing full-time.

Her bestselling Conard County series has won the hearts of readers worldwide, and it's no wonder, given her own approach to life and love. As she says: "Life is the biggest romantic adventure of all—and if you're open and aware, the most marvelous things are just waiting to be discovered."

To Mom, who got me started.
I will always miss you.

Chapter 1

Deputy Constance Halloran drove along the U.S. highway toward Conard City, taking her time, keeping an eye on traffic, glad her shift was almost over.

Spring had settled over the county, greening it with recent rains, filling the air with the fragrance of wildflowers and the scent she thought of as *green*. With her window rolled down, the aroma wafted into her car, earth's special perfume.

Today had been a lazy day, an easy shift. She'd had only one call about a minor theft at one of the ranches; then she'd spent most of the day patrolling her sector. She hadn't written any speeding tickets, which was unusual. Even the traffic seemed to be enjoying a case of spring fever.

Maybe she would light the barbecue tonight and make some hamburgers. Sophie, her seven-year-old daughter, loved grilled hamburgers beyond everything, and loved the opportunity to eat outside at their porch table almost as much. Of course, the evenings could still get chilly, but a sweater would do.

The idea pleased her, and she began to hum a lilting melody. A semi passed her from the opposite direction and flashed his lights in a friendly manner. Connie flashed back, her smile broadening. Some days it felt good just to be alive.

Another mile down the road, she spotted a man standing on the shoulder, thumb out. At once she put on her roof lights, gave one whoop of her siren and pulled over until he was square in the view of her dash camera. He dropped his arm and waited for her.

A couple of cars passed as she radioed dispatch with her position and the reason for her stop.

"Got it, Connie," Velma said, her smoke-frogged voice cracking. "You be careful, hear?"

"I always am."

Glancing over to make sure she wouldn't be opening her door into traffic, Connie climbed out and approached the man.

As she drew closer, she realized he looked scruffy and exotic all at once. Native American, she registered instantly. Long black hair with a streak of gray fell to his shoulders. He also had a beard, unusually thick for someone of his genetic background. Dark eyes looked back at her. The thousand-yard stare. She'd seen it before.

For an instant she wondered if he was mentally ill; then her mind pieced together the conglomeration of clothing he wore, and she identified him as a soldier, or maybe a veteran. His pants were made of the new digitized camouflage fabric, but his jacket was the old olive drab. As she approached, he let a backpack slip from his shoulder to the ground, revealing the collar of his cammie shirt, and she saw the black oak leaf of a major.

At once some of her tension eased. "I'm sorry, sir," she said courteously, "but hitchhiking is illegal."

He nodded, his gaze leaving her and scanning the surrounding countryside. "Sorry, I forgot. Been out of the country."

"I guessed that. Whereabouts?"

His inky gaze returned to her. "Afghanistan. I'll just keep walking."

"No," she said impulsively, breaking all the rules in an instant. "I'll drive you to town. How come you don't have a car?"

Something like amusement, just a hint, flickered swiftly across his face. "I need to be home a while longer before I'll be comfortable behind the wheel."

She let that go, sensing the story behind it wasn't something he was about to share. "Well, hop in. I'm going off shift, so unless something happens, I'll have you in town in twenty minutes."

"Thanks."

He hefted his backpack and followed her to the car. Breaking more rules, she let him sit in front with her, rather than in the safer backseat cage. Even in the large

SUVs the department preferred, he seemed too big. Over six feet, easily, and sturdily built.

She reached for her microphone and called the dispatcher. "I'm back on the road, Velma, on my way in. I'm giving someone a ride."

Velma tutted loudly. "You know you shouldn't."

"It's a special case."

"Whatever." Velma sounded disgusted in the way of a woman used to having her good advice ignored.

Connie signed off and smiled at her passenger. "Velma is the department's mother."

He nodded, saying nothing. A few seconds later they were back on the road, heading down the highway toward town. They passed a herd of cattle on a gentle slope, grazing amicably alongside a group of deer. In places the barbed-wire fences were totally hidden in a tangle of tumbleweed. Indian paintbrush dotted the roadside with scarlet and orange, as if the colors had been scattered by a giant hand.

"It's beautiful country," Connie remarked. "Are you staying or just passing through?"

"A bit of both."

"You have friends here?"

"Sort of. Some folks I want to see, anyway."

She opened her mouth to ask who, then swallowed the words. He didn't seem to want to talk much— maybe with good reason, considering where he'd been. She thought of Billy Joe Yuma, her cousin Wendy's husband, and the problems he still suffered sometimes from Vietnam. This guy's wounds had to be fresher.

When she spoke again, it was to ask something less invasive. "Ever been here before?"

"No."

Well, that gambit wasn't going to work. Stifling a sigh, she gave her attention back to the road and tried to ignore the man beside her. If he stayed in town for more than twenty-four hours, someone would learn something about him and word would pass faster than wildfire. The county had grown quite a bit in the past fifteen years, but it hadn't grown much. People still knew everything about their neighbors, and strangers still attracted a lot of curiosity and speculation.

However, it went against the grain for her to treat a stranger with silence. Around here, folks generally made strangers feel welcome.

"I can take you to a motel if you want."

"Sheriff's office is fine."

"Okay." A scattering of houses near the road announced that Conard City now lay less than ten miles ahead. "My uncle used to be sheriff here," she said by way of keeping a friendly conversation going.

"Yeah?"

At last a sign of curiosity. "He retired a couple of years ago," she explained. "He and my aunt are in South America and are later going on a cruise to Antarctica. It blows my mind to even think of it."

That elicited a chuckle. "It wouldn't be my choice."

"Mine, either, right now. Maybe when I retire I'll see things differently."

"You never know."

She tossed him another glance and saw that he appeared a bit more relaxed.

"So," he said after a moment, "you followed in your uncle's footsteps?"

"Eventually. I grew up in Laramie. Then I moved to Denver."

"How'd that work out?"

"Well, I got my degree, got married, got divorced, decided I didn't like the big bad world all that much and came back to be a deputy."

"What's that like?"

"I love it." She glanced at him again, wondering what had suddenly unlocked the key to his mouth. But he seemed to have gone away again, looking out the windows, watching intently. So on guard. Expecting trouble at any instant.

And there were no magic words to cure that. Nothing but time would do that, if even that could succeed.

"I worked as a cop in the city," she said after a moment. "It's better here."

"Why?"

"Less crime. More helping people."

"I can see that."

She reckoned he could.

"So do you like your new sheriff?"

"Gage Dalton," she supplied. "Yeah. He can be hard to get to know, but once you do, he's great. He used to be DEA, then he came here and my dad hired him as a criminologist. We never had one before."

"That is small-town."

She smiled. "Yeah. It's great."

They reached the edge of town, and soon were driving along Main Street toward the courthouse square and the storefront sheriff's office. On the way, she pointed out the City Diner.

"Eat there if you want rib-sticking food. Despite the sign out front, everyone calls it Maude's diner. You won't find high-class service, but if you're not worried about cholesterol, sugar or salt, there's no better place to get a meal or a piece of pie."

"I'll remember that."

She pulled into her slot in front of the office and turned off the ignition. Before he climbed out, she turned in her seat to face him directly. "I'm Connie Halloran," she said.

"Ethan. Thanks for the ride."

Then he slipped out of the vehicle with his backpack and began to stride toward the diner. She watched him until he disappeared inside, then shook her head and climbed out, locking the car behind her.

Inside the office, Velma arched thin brows at her. "You're still alive, I see."

"I'm not totally stupid."

"Just save the excuses until your uncle gets back."

Connie shook her head and hung her keys from the rack near Velma's dispatch station. "I'm all grown up, Velma."

"That won't matter a flea dropping on a compost heap if anything happens to you. I don't want to be the one explaining to Nate what you did."

Connie leaned over the counter, grinning at the older woman. "I'm armed and dangerous, Velma."

All that earned was a snort. "Damn near everyone around here is armed. It don't keep bad things from happening."

"Nothing bad happened. Now I'm going to sign out and go home to grill burgers for my daughter and my mother."

But Velma stopped her. "Who'd you give a ride to?"

"Some guy named Ethan. He says he has some friends around here."

"And you believe that?"

Connie sighed. "Why wouldn't I? He's wearing a major's oak leaf on his shirt collar, and he says he just got back from Afghanistan. Not your ordinary bad-guy disguise."

Velma's expression soured. "For somebody who patrolled the streets in Denver, you're awfully trusting."

"No, I just know how well I can take care of myself."

Velma's snort followed her out the door.

Chapter 2

Gage Dalton, Conard County's new sheriff—for three years now, which he guessed meant he would always be the new sheriff—sat at his desk reviewing reports, his scarred face smiling faintly as he remembered how Nate Tate used to complain about the paperwork. Nate had been sheriff for thirty-five years, a long time to complain about paperwork. As for Gage, he would count himself lucky if twenty years from now he was still the new sheriff and still doing paperwork.

Not that folks gave him a hard time or anything. It was, he supposed, just their way of distinguishing him from Nate. He signed another report and added it to the stack of completed work.

Not much happened in this county on a routine basis. Cattle disappeared or were killed under strange circumstances. That whole cattle-mutilation thing still hovered around, leaving questions whose answers never entirely satisfied the ranchers.

Break-ins, vandalism—more of that over the past few years as the county grew and bored youngsters got ideas from movies, television and gangsta rap. Although, to his way of thinking, the growing size of the younger population probably meant that, percent-age-wise, there was no more crime than ever.

There were new jobs, though. When he'd first moved here fifteen years ago, the county had been losing many of its young folks to brighter city lights. Then the lights here had grown a bit brighter when a semiconductor plant was set up outside town. Easier work than ranching. Good wages. Folks had moved in, and more kids stayed, especially now that they had a local college, too.

Small changes with outsize impact. Nothing threat-ened the old way of life here yet, but it sure was odd to see kids wearing saggy, beltless, shapeless pants, as if the whole world wanted to see their underwear, instead of boot-cut jeans and ropers. Among the younger set, the cowboy hat had been completely replaced by the ball cap. Sometimes Gage grinned, because it was all familiar to him from the days before he moved here. It had just taken longer to arrive than he had, that was all.

Velma buzzed him on the intercom. "Sheriff? There's a man here looking for Micah."

Gage didn't hesitate. "Send him back."

Maybe he remained overly cautious from his DEA days, but Gage was protective of his deputies, their addresses and their whereabouts. Velma's description had spoken volumes. She hadn't given the visitor a name, which meant he wasn't local. Gage went instantly on guard.

A half minute later, a tall dark man appeared in Gage's doorway. Gage experienced an instant of recognition so fleeting it was gone before he could nail it down.

"Come in," he said to the stranger, rising to offer his hand.

The man took it and shook firmly, giving Gage a chance to study him. His first guess was Native American, but the thick beard threw him off. Coppery skin tone, but that could be from the sun. Chambray shirt and jeans.

"Gage Dalton," he said. "Have we met before?"

The man shook his head. "Major Ethan Parish."

At once Gage stilled. He studied the man even more closely, and now the instant of recognition made sense. "You look a bit like him. Related?"

Ethan nodded.

"Well, take a seat."

The two men sat facing each other across the expanse of the old wood desk with its stacks of papers.

"Does Micah know you're here?" Gage asked.

"No."

"I see." Gage drummed his fingers on the desk for just a moment. He recognized the look in Ethan

Parish's eyes. Micah still showed it on occasion, as did Billy Joe Yuma, the county's rescue pilot. He had also seen the look on the faces of his fellow DEA agents when they'd been on the streets too long. Sometimes he saw it in his own mirror.

"Look," he said after a moment. "If Micah doesn't know you're here, I don't feel I should be telling you how to find him. Maybe you should call him."

"This isn't something I want to do on the phone."

"Why not?"

Ethan Parish hesitated, looking past Gage as if debating how much to tell.

"Tell you what," Gage said after a few moments. "Tell me who you are. Something about yourself."

"Marine recon, special operations. One tour in Iraq, two in Afghanistan. Other things I can't tell you about. I won't be going back. Medical discharge."

"You were wounded?"

"More than once."

Gage nodded. "I'm sorry."

Ethan Parish merely looked at him. "I'm better off than many."

Gage nodded again. "Still walking."

Ethan nodded once. "And talking. Anyway, I'll be officially discharged within the next six months."

"Need a job?"

"If I stay here."

Gage rubbed his chin and settled back in his chair. "How's Micah fit in the picture?"

Ethan's mouth tightened.

"Look, you know about protecting your men. I'm no different."

That seemed to cause a shift in the man facing him. At last Ethan relaxed a hair. "This can't get out."

"Believe me, I know how to keep a secret. I was undercover DEA before I came here."

That did the trick. "Micah Parish doesn't know it, but he's my father."

Gage froze. "Oh, hell," he said finally. "This could raise a real storm."

"That's why I don't want it getting out until I talk to him."

"I can sure understand that." Gage paused to think again. "Okay," he said finally. "Tell you what I'll do. Micah's on his day off, so I'll drive you out to his ranch. But you better not tell his wife who you are before you get a chance to talk to him in private."

"That's how I was hoping to handle it."

"Then we see eye-to-eye. Come on, let's go. You can think up a cover story while we drive."

That afternoon, Connie's world blew up. It happened the way such things do, utterly without warning, and in an instant that was otherwise utterly benign.

On her day off, she always had plenty to do. Her mother, disabled by a severe fall several years ago, helped as much as she could, but being stuck in a wheelchair severely limited her activities. In many ways she created extra work for Connie, but it was work she didn't mind, because she didn't know how she would have been able to hold a job and care for Sophie properly at the same time without her mother there.

Sophie had reached the amazing age of seven, when girls start to act like little mothers, developing a streak of independence and becoming downright bossy. So far, Sophie's imitation of motherhood had proved more amusing than anything else, although Connie suspected that at some point they would need to have a discussion before the girl alienated all her friends by bossing them around.

"Perfectly normal," Connie's mother said. "All girls do it. It'd be worse if she had a brother."

"I suppose."

Connie climbed down from the ladder where she'd been spackling a small crack in the ceiling. Some major problems had begun to brew in the old house, but she couldn't afford to deal with them yet. "Want some coffee, Mom?"

"I'll never pass up a cup of coffee," Julia answered. "You know that. You don't even have to ask."

"Sophie should be home soon," Connie remarked as she washed both her hands and the spackling knife at the sink. "She'd better hurry. It looks like we might get a storm."

Julia turned her wheelchair so she could look out the tall window over the sink. "So it does. I wanted to ask you something."

Connie grabbed a towel to dry her hands and turned, leaning back against the counter. She raised her eyebrows. "I always hate it when you say that."

"Why?"

"Because it always means it's not an ordinary question."

Julia laughed. "Well, you're too old for me to send to your room, so I think you're safe."

Connie laughed, too. Just at the edge of hearing, she heard a rumble of thunder. "What is it?"

"I want to get Sophie a dog."

"Oh. Is that all?" Connie draped the towel on the rack by the sink.

Julia cocked her head to one side. "I don't know how to take that."

"Well, take it that I'm listening. Why do you want to get her a dog?"

"She's been asking for one. And Pru's dachshund just had a litter."

"A little dog, huh?"

"Well…" Julia drew the word out.

"Well, what?"

"Pru's not sure who the father is. And some of the pups have pretty big feet."

Connie couldn't help the laugh that escaped her. "Do you know what an image that is? A dachshund with those short, short legs and huge feet?"

Julia laughed, too.

"Sort of like a basset hound," Connie remarked. "Long, low and short. It's okay if she gets a dog, Mom. But she's got to take care of it."

"I was thinking it would be a chance to use her mothering urges on something besides her friends."

"Every little bit helps. Just be sure you're comfortable with the idea, because you know Sophie is going to forget at times."

"I'm a great reminder."

"Nag, Mom. The word is nag."

They were still laughing together when Sophie burst into the room with her best friend, Jody, out of breath and looking scared.

"Mom! Mom! A man tried to talk to us when we were walking home! He chased us!"

Chapter 3

As Gage's SUV drove up the rutted drive to Micah's house, neither man said a word. Then a two-story house with a gabled roof came into view, a barn not far away. A woman was visible outside the house, hanging laundry. She was small and blond, looking as delicate as a flower petal.

"That's his wife, Faith. The school bus won't bring their kids home for another half hour, at least. I'll wait for you unless you tell me otherwise."

Ethan nodded. His face felt chiseled from stone. Gage wheeled into the large yard, waving at Faith as he did so. She waved back, one hand holding a shapeless piece of laundry.

"There you go," Gage said. His hands were tight on the wheel as he stopped.

Ethan paused for a moment, then climbed out.

He had no idea what to expect. Faith froze like a frightened deer when she saw him. Statuelike, she watched him approach. He did so slowly, not wanting to frighten her more, wondering why she was frightened at all when Gage was here.

But then, in an instant, she dropped the laundry she held and gasped, "You look just like Micah when he was younger."

Ethan paused awkwardly. "We're related."

"I thought so." Then she astonished him by hurrying toward him and wrapping him in a hug. "This is wonderful," she said. "Absolutely wonderful!"

A moment later she stepped back, holding his arms as she looked up at him. Her smile was wide and welcoming, and then perplexity entered her eyes, followed by the wavering of her smile.

"I'm sorry I shocked you," Ethan said quickly.

Faith shook her head. Biting her lower lip, she continued to search his face. "You look so much like him. You're not just a cousin, are you?"

She said it more like a statement than a question. Ethan hesitated, not sure whether to lie, and that hesitation apparently gave him away.

"You're…you're his son, aren't you?"

Slowly Ethan nodded. He hadn't expected to feel gut-punched, hadn't expected to feel his stomach quiver nervously. He had thought very little could fill him with fear any longer. But he felt fear now, as if everything rested on this small woman's decision.

There was an instant, just an instant, when she seemed to gather herself; then her smile steadied again. "That's wonderful. I'm surprised he never mentioned you."

"He doesn't know."

She nodded, almost a rocking movement. "I see. Well, then, this will certainly be a great day for him."

"I wish I were sure of that."

A little laugh escaped her. "I am."

"You're not upset?"

She tilted her head to one side. "Micah was forty-two when I met him. I'd have to be a foolish woman indeed to think I was his first and only love."

Tension seeped out of Ethan, allowing him to smile at last. "Thank you."

"Come inside. He's in the upper pasture checking on the sheep, but he'll be back soon." She turned and gestured to Gage to join them.

"I'm just the transportation," Gage called. "Don't let me get in the way."

"You're never in the way. But if you want to go home to Emma, we can take care of him."

"You're sure?"

"Absolutely."

Gage waved and drove back down the long ranch road, trailing a cloud of dust in his wake.

Leaving the laundry, Faith took Ethan's hand and gently urged him toward the door. "This is remarkable," she said. "Absolutely remarkable."

He thought the only truly remarkable thing was that this woman, who had never seen him before, was so ready to accept him and take him in.

Inside, she motioned him to the kitchen table. "Coffee?"

"I'd love some."

She put a pot on the stove to brew, then sat facing him, her eyes drinking in every detail. "It's strange, but I feel like it's fifteen years ago and I'm meeting Micah for the first time."

"I didn't know I looked so much like him."

"Except for the beard." She nodded, her fingers twisting together. "So tell me about yourself, about your mother. Or you can wait for Micah, so you don't have to do it twice."

"I…" He hesitated. Then he said frankly, "I'm not used to talking about myself much."

"Then let me tell you about us." She seemed comfortable with that, and he was grateful. "We met and married about fifteen years ago. I have a daughter by a previous marriage, and together we have two daughters, twins. Micah saved my life." Her eyes darkened with memory, but he didn't ask, allowing her to tell her story in her own way.

She shook herself a bit, then smiled. "You also have an uncle here. He and his family live on a ranch a few miles from here."

"An uncle?"

"Micah's brother, Gideon. They didn't grow up together, but you'd never guess it now. You'll like him,

I'm sure. He's a born horse whisperer, and he mainly trains and breeds horses these days. His wife is also a deputy, Sara Ironheart."

"Interesting family."

"To put it mildly." Faith smiled. "And now we have you. I'm the only ordinary person in the lot."

"Ordinary?"

She shrugged. "I've never done anything special. Everyone else has."

"I don't consider anything I've done special."

"Really?" She didn't look as if she quite believed him. "There's something about you that makes me think otherwise. Something like Micah. You've had a hard life."

"Everyone has."

"Not like that." She reached out unexpectedly and patted the back of his hand. "You can talk to Micah about it. He's the most understanding man in the world."

Connie sat both girls at the table while her mother set about making some hot chocolate to soothe them. But Connie wasn't about to be soothed.

Jody was crying, and Connie gave her a tissue. "I'll call your mom, Jody, then I'll drive you home, okay?"

The little girl nodded and sniffled.

After calling Jody's mother, telling her nothing but that Jody was going to be with Sophie for a bit, she joined them at the table.

"Now tell me everything. Every single thing you

remember," Connie said gently. But she wasn't feeling gentle at all. At that moment she felt as close to murder as she ever had, even when her ex-husband had beaten her.

"It was a man in an old car," Sophie said. She was scared, but not as scared as Jody, for some reason.

"He followed us," Jody said, hiccupping.

"Followed you? How?"

"He drove real slow," Sophie said. "We kinda noticed it, so we looked."

Connie's heart slammed. "And then?"

Jody sniffled again. "He saw us looking at him, and he called out for Sophie."

"By name?"

"Yeah," Sophie said. "But I remembered what you said about strangers. So we started to run away from the car, and he yelled he just wanted to talk to me." Her eyes seemed to fill her face. "We got really scared when he started to drive after us, so me and Jody cut across the backyards."

For an instant, terror struck Connie so hard she felt light-headed. Her mind raced at top speed, trying to deal with dread and speculations, all of them enough to make her nearly sick.

Connie's mother spoke. "Come get your hot chocolate, girls. It's ready."

Connie grabbed for the phone receiver on the wall and dialed the emergency number. Velma's familiar voice became an anchor.

"What's up, honey?"

"A stranger went after my daughter and her friend. I need someone at my house right now."

Velma disconnected without another word. Slowly Connie hung up the phone and attempted to gather herself. When she felt composed enough, she turned back to the girls.

"What did he look like?" she asked as the girls politely took mugs from Julia, who then began to put cookies on a plate for them.

"Ugly," Sophie answered. "He had a dirty beard. His clothes were old."

Connie's thoughts immediately flew to the stranger she'd driven into town just yesterday. Ethan, that was his name. But his beard hadn't been dirty. Nor had he been wearing old clothes. But who knew what he might be wearing today?

"Did he say anything else?"

"No," Sophie said, returning to the table. "We ran away."

"Can you tell me anything about his car?"

Jody sniffed away the last of her tears and came back to the table with her mug. Julia put the plate of cookies in front of the girls.

"Brown," Sophie announced. "But not dark like a crayon."

"Was it big or small?"

"Not as big as a sheriff car, but bigger than our car."

That was quite a range. "Anything else you can remember?"

Both girls shook their heads.

"Okay, you enjoy your cookies and cocoa while we wait for a deputy."

By that point, both girls were more interested in their cookies than in what had scared them. Ah, for the resilience of the young, she thought.

Because she was still angry and terrified. She wanted to grab her gun and go hunting for this man who had scared her daughter. She wanted to make sure he never again frightened a child.

Which was precisely why she joined them at the table and tried to smile, tried to cover all the protective, angry feelings inside her.

"It's going to be okay. Another deputy is coming to help, and we'll find him."

God willing.

Chapter 4

Gage was halfway back to the office when he got the radio call from Velma.

"Connie's all upset. I'm sending Sara over there."

"What happened?"

"Some stranger approached her daughter."

"I'm on my way."

"Uh, boss?"

At least Velma didn't refer to him as the new boss. "What?"

"Those kids are already terrified."

"Meaning?" He thought instantly of his scarred face, of the shiny skin where the bomb that had killed his family had burned his cheek. There had been a time when he'd thought he ought to wear a mask like the phantom in *Phantom of the Opera,* so he wouldn't scare children, but surprisingly few, if any, kids were scared of him. Certainly not around here.

"Well, I was just thinking," Velma said, "too many cops all at once…"

"Might make them feel safer," Gage finished. "I'm on my way." With that he switched on his light bar and hit the accelerator hard. If some creep was hanging around, the sooner they got him, the better.

Micah got home before Ethan had finished half a cup of coffee. He walked in the door, hat in hand, and froze almost as soon as he was inside. His dark gaze flicked from his wife to Ethan, then back.

Ethan rose to his feet and stared at the man he had been told was his father. There was an instant when he felt almost as if he were looking in a mirror, but only an instant, for almost at once he saw the differences. His face was weathered, but Micah's was substantially more so. His own jaw was a little squarer, and he was the taller by almost an inch. Less muscular, though. Running around the Afghan mountains on very little food had made him leaner, rangier.

But then gaze met gaze, and there was an instant of almost preternatural recognition that pinned them both to the spot.

"Micah," Faith said. "Micah?" Her husband looked at her. "This is Ethan Parish."

Micah's gaze shot back to the younger man. "Parish?"

"My mother was Ella Birdsong."

"Ella…" Micah repeated the name slowly, almost doubtfully. Then his face darkened. "She left me when I was ordered overseas on an extended op. I never knew where she went."

"She told me."

"She never said…"

"That she was pregnant," Ethan finished. "I know. She told me that, too. There's no blame here."

After a moment, Micah nodded. Then he advanced farther into the kitchen and reached out to shake Ethan's hand. "Good to meet you," he said, as he might have said to any stranger.

"Sit down, love," Faith said. "I'll get you some coffee. The kids will be home from school soon."

Micah nodded again, put his hat on a peg, then sat at the table. His gaze remained fixed on Ethan. "How's your mother?"

"She died three years ago."

"I'm sorry."

Ethan nodded. "I am, too. She was a good woman. I don't know why she never told you. She just said it was for the best."

"I know she wasn't happy about me being special ops."

"Then maybe that's all it was."

Micah thanked Faith for the coffee and took a sip, still studying his son. "What have you been doing?"

Ethan almost heard the unspoken question, *Why didn't you come sooner?* But he chose to take his father's words at face value. "Marine recon," he said.

"Iraq? Afghanistan?"

"Both." Ethan hesitated. "I just got out of Walter Reed. I'll be discharged soon. Medical."

Micah's face tightened. "I'm sorry."

"I'm better off than most."

"I can see that."

Faith stirred. "Why don't I go out to meet the kids at the bus? So you two can have some time. Ethan, you're welcome to stay with us."

He looked at her. "No, thank you, ma'am. I don't think I'm ready for that."

"If you ever change your mind, the invitation will be open." Then she grabbed a sweater off the peg beside Micah's hat and slipped out through the screen door. It slapped closed behind her.

The two men stared at one another, tied by blood, separated by a gulf of years.

"I probably should have called first," Ethan said finally.

Micah shook his head. "It's a surprise any way you want to announce it."

"I suppose it is."

"Well, hell." Micah stood up from the table and walked once around the kitchen before going to stand at the screen door, looking out. "I knew," he said finally.

"Knew what?"

"I knew you were out there."

"What? She told you?"

"No." He turned slowly and looked at Ethan. "I just had a feeling. Like a piece of me was out there some- where. I always wondered if it would turn up."

Ethan turned his chair so that he could look straight at his father. He crossed his legs. "My mother said you weirded her out sometimes."

At that Micah chuckled. "She didn't like the shaman in me."

"She didn't like it in me, either."

Understanding suddenly crackled in the air between them, like lightning, a feeling almost strong enough to make hair stand on end.

"You're my son," Micah said. His tone brooked no doubt.

"I am."

Micah returned to the table. "Then we've got a lot of time to make up for."

Connie stood outside with Gage, her arms wrapped tightly around herself. Cops were cruising all over town and the surrounding countryside, looking for the stranger who had accosted the girls.

"Bigger than your car and smaller than mine isn't much of a description," Gage remarked.

"No. But a beard. I thought immediately of the guy I gave a ride to yesterday."

Gage faced her directly. "Who was that?"

"I thought he was a major. He had the rank on his shirt collar. Native American, but with a beard."

Gage shook his head. "Not him."

"How do you know?" Her voice held an edge.

"Because while Sophie and Jody were being approached by this stranger, I was driving Ethan Parish out to Micah's place."

"Ethan *Parish?*"

Gage nodded. "Big guy, kinda lean, back from Afghanistan."

Reluctantly Connie nodded. "So it's not going to be that easy."

"Afraid not."

"What do we do now?"

"You know the drill," Gage said quietly. "You escort Sophie to and from school. I'll make sure you have time to do it. And if it's not you, it'll be me or one of the others, okay?"

"And Jody?"

"She doesn't seem to have been the target, but I'll tell her folks they need to watch her, too. And I'm going to double the in-town patrols so we can keep an eye on all the kids as they walk to and from school."

"Good idea. Maybe he just happened to know Sophie's name."

"Maybe." Gage looked past her, scanning the area. "If we don't find him, all this activity will probably scare him on his way."

"Probably." But Connie still couldn't relax. "All the parents need to know."

"Of course. The school is already taking care of that."

"Good." Connie sighed. "Gage, I'm scared to death."

"I don't blame you. But this isn't New York or Chicago, Connie. There aren't a lot of places to hide."

"In town, anyway." She suppressed a shudder. "I promised Jody's mother I'd bring her home."

"I'll do it. You just stay here with Sophie. I'll leave Sarah here, too. The rest of us will keep searching."

"Thanks, Gage."

He surprised her with a quick hug, then gave her a straight stare. "You know this whole town is going to be watching now. Sophie will be safe."

"Yes. Yes." But something in her couldn't quite believe that. The unthinkable had happened. And it had happened to her daughter.

She stayed outside in the gathering dusk while Gage retrieved Jody and put her in his car. Only then did she go back inside the brightly lit kitchen where her daughter, mother and Deputy Sarah Ironheart were sitting.

She tried to smile brightly for Sophie's sake. "I was going to grill burgers again tonight," she said, "but I don't feel like it anymore. How about we try ordering from that new Italian place? They deliver."

Sophie was over her fear now, and the idea of pizza thrilled her. So easy, sometimes, to be a child.

Not so easy to be a mother. Connie didn't sleep a wink that night.

Chapter 5

Everyone in the county knew about Sophie's encounter by morning. Even Ethan could tell something was going on as he walked into town from the motel to get breakfast at Maude's. He noted that he was getting a lot of suspicious looks he hadn't received even the day before, and by the time he sat down at a table in the diner, he knew he was under surveillance.

His skin crawled with it. He waited for Maude to come to his table, pretending not to notice, but every nerve ending in his body was wound tighter than a spring. Hyper-alert, on guard, half expecting a bomb or a gunshot.

What he got, instead, was a menu, and a few minutes

later Gage Dalton entered the restaurant. Gage stood looking around the room and announced easily, "This man is *not* the man who approached Sophie Halloran yesterday. Leave him alone."

The eyes shifted away, conversation resumed, and in seconds Ethan had heard enough to understand the basics of what had the whole town acting as if it was under attack.

Gage joined him at the table, and Maude returned for their orders.

"Steak and eggs, over easy," Gage said to Maude.

She snorted. "Like you have to tell me that." Then she looked at Ethan.

"Same here," he said.

"So what's your name?" Maude demanded. "I don't like to call people 'hey, you.'"

He rustled up a smile. "Ethan."

Maude nodded. "You want coffee with that?"

"Always."

Another nod, then she grabbed the menu and stomped away.

"Our Maude," said Gage, "has great charm. It does take some getting used to."

"She's harmless enough," Ethan said.

"Depends on your point of comparison."

"So what exactly happened yesterday? I was half-sure I'd get shot while I was walking into town this morning."

"Remember the deputy who gave you a ride the other day? Connie Halloran?"

"Yeah."

"Some stranger approached her daughter in a car and called her over by name."

"I gathered that somebody had tried to abduct a kid, but I didn't know it was *her* kid."

Gage shook his head. "The rumor mill is in high gear. No abduction attempt, though. At least, not overtly. The guy wanted to talk to the girl."

"That's creepy enough."

Gage leaned forward, lowering his voice. "When Micah came in this morning, he suggested I take you on."

Ethan was startled. "Take me on?"

"As a deputy. At least temporarily."

"But why?"

"He seems to feel you're fresher at dealing with threats than the rest of us." Gage grinned. "He's right, you know. Whatever we used to be, we're all small-town cops now."

Ethan nodded slowly, turning the idea over in his head. He, too, kept his voice low. "You want me to protect the girl?"

"Sort of."

Ethan waited patiently. He was good at that from years of sitting in out-of-the-way places waiting, waiting, waiting for his target. For information. For whatever.

"The thing is, what if this guy isn't really a stranger?"

Ethan's brow creased. "What do you mean?"

"Sophie didn't recognize the guy, but she's only seven. Anyway, everyone has it fixed in their heads that this guy is someone from outside the county. What if he's not? They'll dismiss anyone they know, even if he does something suspicious."

"I see what you mean."

"Now maybe Sophie's his target. Or maybe he just happens to like little blond girls and goes for another one. Whichever way, if Farmer Sam sees Rancher Jesse talking to a little girl, he's not going to get suspicious. Because they're neighbors."

"I read you."

Gage smiled. "Micah said you'd help."

"He did, did he?"

Gage's smile broadened. "I always wanted another Micah Parish on my staff." He laughed and leaned back to let Maude pour their coffee, then put their plates in front of them. After she moved away, he leaned in again, keeping his voice well below the level of surrounding conversation. "We'll go over to the office after breakfast. It's time to plan."

"I didn't say I'd do it."

Gage's smile faded as he studied the younger man. After a bit he said, "You'll do it. You're not the kind to walk away."

Ethan walked back to the sheriff's office with Gage. Throughout breakfast, only a few more words had passed between them, either, because neither man was much of a talker or because too many ears were listening.

Ethan had come this way looking for something of himself, something that wasn't connected to the years in Afghanistan and Iraq. Whoever, whatever, he'd been before was gone. Now, about to return to civilian life, he needed new anchors. Experience had taught him to deal with events that came out of the blue, often hectic, usually unstoppable and always initially confusing. It took a lot to throw him offstride.

But right now he felt very much offstride. He wasn't exactly sure what he'd expected coming out here, but this sure as hell wasn't it. He hadn't expected events to rise around him like quicksand again.

Protect a little girl? How could he say no?

"Velma," Gage said as they passed the dispatcher's desk, "Ethan here is going to be working with us. And I don't want anyone outside the department to know that for a while."

She snorted and blew smoke through her nostrils. A cigarette dangled from her left hand, ash hanging precariously. "Like that's gonna happen."

"You heard me. I know you can keep a secret."

They were already turning into Gage's office as Velma called after them, "It won't be me who lets the cat out."

Gage half smiled. "That woman is such an icon at that desk that if she ever passes on, we're going to have to put a statue of her there."

Ethan returned the half smile and settled into the chair he'd occupied only the day before. Gage rounded the desk, running his fingers through his prematurely gray hair, and sat.

"Help me here," he said. "We need to run surveillance. Keep an eye on Sophie in a way that doesn't overly restrict her. Keep an eye on the other kids. Because what we don't know here is whether she was a specific target or a target of opportunity. He could know the names of dozens of kids."

"Certainly possible if he's a local."

"The schools will be on lockdown all day. No students will be allowed out. Parents are being advised to pick up their kids at school or at bus stops. But that still leaves after school."

Ethan nodded. "My bet is that if the guy hasn't moved on, he's not going to try anything until the heat lessens. Just walking from the motel to the diner, I could tell you're on high alert."

"Are you saying we should stop?"

"I'm saying you need to be less visible." Ethan leaned forward. "If the guy hasn't moved on, you need to surveil in a way that will give him the guts to make a move. Otherwise, once things have been quiet for a week or so, you're going back to your normal routine and he's coming out of the woodwork."

"I was thinking that, too." Gage rubbed his chin. "But if we're facing a local, then all my deputies are well-known. It won't matter if they're in or out of uniform."

Ethan nodded slowly. "In Iraq and Afghanistan, I never removed my uniform. I knew I was walking around with a target painted on me."

"Which means?"

"You still have to be there. Just gradually lessen your patrols so it looks like you're going back to normal. But make sure everyone in the department knows you're not. That they have to leave what look like gaps, but only briefly. Sort of like fanning out but making sure you can always manage crossfire, if you follow."

Gage nodded. "And nobody gets in and out of town without being noted."

"Yes. So basically, you widen your perimeter, let it become porous, but not so porous you can't close it up fast."

"Makes sense. It'll take a little time to put it into practice."

"Yeah, it will," Ethan agreed, "but you don't want to relax your patrols too quickly, anyway. Never signal the enemy that you're laying a trap."

Gage rose and poured two cups of coffee from the drip coffeemaker on a rickety side table. He passed one to Ethan.

"I've got one more thing," he said as he resumed his seat. "It involves you directly."

Ethan arched a brow, waiting.

"Nobody in town knows who you are yet, especially since you registered at the hotel under the name Birdsong. So, I called Micah about this, and he agrees. He and Faith won't say anything about you. And I want you to move in with Connie."

Ethan stiffened. "Hold on there."

Gage shook his head. "It will work. You're an old

friend of Connie's from Denver. She decided to ask you to stay with her."

A million alarm bells sounded in Ethan's head. "What good will that do? The guy isn't going to try to steal the little girl out of her bed."

"No, but it will make it easier for you to keep an eye on her, and nobody would know you were working for me. So if you happen to be seen around Sophie, you have a cover story. Otherwise…"

Otherwise pretend he was back in the mountains, on recon. Passing like a ghost through all kinds of danger. Except the danger here wasn't directed at him.

Things inside him that had just begun to loosen once again clenched like fists. He was painted, man. He was always painted.

He put his coffee down. "You better make sure the lady is okay with this. Because I'm not sure I am."

"She will be," Gage said confidently, his face darkening as if with memory. "Parents tend to be willing to do anything to keep their children safe."

Anything, Ethan agreed silently. Anything. He'd sure as hell seen enough of what that meant.

But all too often it resulted in horror that could sear the soul.

Chapter 6

Connie couldn't believe she was standing in a store getting a cell phone for her seven-year-old daughter. It seemed surreal. She'd never wanted one for herself, even after the technology arrived in the county, complete with two different carriers to choose from. Of course, she was hooked up by radio to the department, so a cell phone had struck her as just another intrusion.

Not anymore. Now it meant safety. Safety for Sophie. Her daughter would now have an immediate means of calling her mother or calling the sheriff. As Connie scanned the various plans, she started to choose the cheapest one with a minimum of minutes until she realized the obvious: Sophie was bound to use the phone to call friends, at least until the novelty wore off. Like parents everywhere, she gave up the fight before it began and protected herself against sky-high charges by purchasing a plan with more minutes than she thought Sophie could possibly use.

She bought a case to protect the phone, one that would loop fully around Sophie's belt, not just clip there. Then she got a phone for herself.

She walked out of the store with her plastic bag, feeling that somehow time had slipped its moorings. Conard City—all of Conard County—had always been a safe place for children, as safe as any place could be. She had the strangest feeling that she had switched centuries, that time had warped and carried her into a frightening new world.

Ridiculous, of course. Her time in Denver had exposed her to all this. But Conard County had in many ways escaped the worst of current times.

Climbing back into her cruiser, she gave herself a mental kick in the butt. How many times had she heard someone say on the TV news, "These things just don't happen in this town"?

They happened everywhere. She knew it then, and she knew it now. The difference, of course, was that her daughter would be the subject of the news story if things didn't work out.

Her radio crackled even before she pulled out of the parking place.

"Get on back to the office, sweetie," Velma said. "Gage needs you. Nothing bad."

A good thing Velma had added that, Connie thought, as she wheeled away from the curb and headed back to the office. Her heart had been caught in mid-slam. *Nothing bad.*

Five minutes later she was sitting in Gage's office with the sheriff and Ethan Parish. Ethan's presence made her uncomfortable in some way. Not fear or anything. Just a sense of discomfort.

"Ethan's joining the department," Gage said.

Connie looked at him. "Congratulations."

He nodded but said nothing.

"I figure it this way," Gage said. "Nobody knows Ethan yet, so nobody's gonna know he's a deputy. So we're going to put the story out that he's an old friend of yours from Denver."

Connie blinked. "Why?"

"Because then he can move into your house and help keep an eye on Sophie."

Connie's chest tightened as if it had suddenly been grabbed and squeezed. Her vision narrowed, and the next thing she knew she was leaning forward, gripping the edge of Gage's desk, panting for air.

She felt, rather than saw, Gage reach her side, felt him grip her shoulders.

"Connie. Connie?"

It was as if she'd been holding it all back, refusing to truly face the reality of the threat to Sophie until this very instant. She'd been scared, she'd been worried, she'd lain awake, but she'd managed to maintain some distance, some control.

In an instant, all that shattered. Reality came home with heart-stopping, mind-pounding force.

"Connie? Do you need medical help?"

She managed a shake of her head. Her voice came out thin, as if she couldn't get any air into it. "Somebody tried to kidnap my daughter."

Gage seemed to understand. He squatted beside her, rubbing her shoulder. "Delayed reaction," he said. "He didn't succeed, Connie. And we're not going to let him succeed. That's why Ethan is going to stay with you. His skills aren't dulled yet by living here. He's in peak form. He'll smell danger before it gets anywhere near Sophie."

She managed a nod, closed her eyes and fought for control. She wouldn't be any good to Sophie like this. She had to stay cool. Keep her wits. Finally she began to breathe again and was able to sit up.

The first thing she did was look at Ethan. "Will you?" she asked. "Do you mind?"

His was a face that didn't smile easily, she could tell, but he gave her a small one now. "Not at all. It's been a while since I felt useful."

"Take the rest of the day, Connie," Gage said, returning to his seat. "Get Ethan settled however you want, get Sophie from school, do whatever you need to so you can cope." For an instant his gaze grew distant. "I know what it's like."

He did, Connie thought. He certainly did.

Together she and Ethan stopped by the motel to pick up his gear; then they drove to her house. Julia's eyes widened when Connie walked into the kitchen with Ethan in tow.

"What's this?" she asked.

"This is Ethan, Mom," Connie answered. "An old friend. He's going to stay with us for a while."

Julia's eyes narrowed. "I can smell a fib from fifty feet."

Ethan surprised Connie by pulling out a chair from the kitchen table so that he and Julia were near eye level. "The truth is, ma'am, I'm here to keep an eye on Sophie. I'm a deputy."

"A new one." Julia's eyes narrowed. "Looks like you've seen some grief."

Ethan shrugged. "The point is, I've been hired as personal protection for your granddaughter. Good enough?"

"Better than nothing."

"Mom!"

Julia looked at her, then back at Ethan. "She hates it when I'm truthful."

"Well," said Ethan, "that wasn't exactly truthful."

"Why not?"

"Because Connie is protection, too. She's not nothing."

At that, Julia cracked a smile. "Okay, then. Go get settled."

"I have a spare bedroom where—" Connie began, but Ethan interrupted her.

"No bedroom," he said. "I'll camp out in the living room. I want to be able to watch the doors."

"Okay." At that point, Connie didn't care. He could perch on the roof if he wanted to, as long as he kept Sophie safe. He tossed his backpack into a corner, out of the way.

"Is it okay if I look around?"

"Help yourself." Connie dropped her plastic bag on the armchair. "I'm going to have to figure out how to use a cell phone by tomorrow morning."

"Why is that?"

"I got one for Sophie."

He nodded. "Good idea."

"It's not something I ever thought I'd do for a seven-year-old."

"Seems smart to me." Then he gave another small smile. "But don't look to me for lessons. I've never had a cell. I'm a radio kind of guy."

"I was a radio kind of girl until yesterday."

She walked him through the house, not that there was much to see. She'd converted the downstairs dining room into a bedroom for her mother. Upstairs, there were three small bedrooms, two with dormers. She used one of those and Sophie the other. The third room, at the back of the house, was cramped, with a low sloping ceiling, but adequate for a twin bed and dresser, if little more.

The house's only bathroom was downstairs, behind the kitchen. The house had all the earmarks of a place that had been built a bit at a time, the mudroom tacked on like an afterthought next to the kitchen. When the weather was bad, it was the way to enter. Otherwise

Connie preferred the side door, between the kitchen and the driveway.

By the time they finished the tour, Julia had a pot of coffee brewing and invited Ethan to join her. He seemed willing enough, so Connie sat with them. She could barely hold still, though. Her eyes kept straying to the clock, counting the minutes until she went to pick up Sophie. Counting the minutes until she could hug her daughter and assure herself that everything was all right.

"What time do we pick her up?" Ethan asked.

"Two-thirty."

"Okay. When I finish this wonderful coffee—" Julia beamed "—I'll walk down to the school and scope things out from cover. After I get back, I think we ought to walk back down together to pick her up."

"Why not take the car?"

"Because if anyone's watching your daughter, I want to know it."

"All right." She wondered how he could be so sure, then decided he'd probably developed a sixth sense for such things where he'd been. It was probably the reason he had survived.

"All right," she said again. "What if I take a ball and we stop at the park on the way back? Let her get some exercise."

He nodded. "Soccer ball?"

"I have one, yes."

"Good. Bring it." He smiled then, a real smile. "Soccer is an international language. It was a great way to break the ice in Afghanistan. All I had to do was take out my ball and start kicking it around, and pretty soon I'd have a dozen or more kids with me, everyone having a great time. Some of my best memories are of kicking a ball around in that dirt and dust."

Connie felt herself smiling with him. She could see the pleasure the memories gave him, and she felt relieved to finally see a softer side to him.

But then her eyes strayed to the clock again. The minutes couldn't possibly move any slower.

Ethan and Connie left early to pick up Sophie at the school. Ethan carried the soccer ball under his arm, and they strolled along as if they had all the time in the world.

Ethan wanted it to look exactly that way. His eyes moved restlessly, noting every detail of the streets, the cars, the houses that lined them. Connie found herself doing pretty much the same thing, seeking anything that seemed out of place.

Ethan spoke. "It must be hard, being a single mother."

"Easier than being married to an abusive jerk. Safer for Sophie and me both."

"I'm sorry. What happened?" He paused. "I guess it's none of my business."

"I don't mind discussing it. I've given some courses in anger management, and I've used my personal experience to illustrate. My ex beat me. As in most cases, at first he was just controlling. It didn't seem too bad.

Then he started to object to my friends. Classic. Cut me off from my support network."

Ethan nodded.

"But even though I was a cop, I couldn't see what was happening to me. It's odd, isn't it, how you can see something happen to someone else but not see the same thing happening to you?"

"I think that's pretty much normal."

"Maybe. Anyway, he undermined my self-confidence, made me feel responsible for everything that went wrong. Then he hit me a couple of times. He always apologized and swore it would never happen again. I was too ashamed to tell anyone. Cop as abused wife. Sheesh. Talk about humiliating."

"So what got you out?"

"When he knocked me down and started kicking me. I was pregnant. That's standard, too. It's like they resent the intrusion, the loss of control. Regardless, I had someone to think about besides myself. That time I didn't take it."

"Good for you."

She shook her head and sighed. "It wasn't pretty. After I managed to get to my feet, I knocked him down and got my gun. After that it was a restraining order and divorce. I never saw him again."

"He couldn't stand up to the gun, huh?"

"I don't know. I mean, it was a dangerous time. Thank God for my buddies on the force. They got me out of the house and into a shelter, and for a long time I never went anywhere alone." She looked over at him.

"That's the time when most women get killed. After they stand up to their abuser and decide to get out. I'll forever be grateful to my fellow officers."

"That's the way it should be. If we don't take care of each other, who will?"

She figured he was thinking about his own unit and a very different set of circumstances. Sometimes one's own scars ached in response to similar scars in others. It was as if like recognized like.

"You're a strong woman," he remarked.

"Sure. That's why I'm coming apart. Sophie needs me, and I'm coming apart."

He touched her arm tentatively, as if afraid of her reaction. "You have to allow those feelings," he said. "The important thing is that you allow them when it's safe to have them. That's what you did in the office this morning. Sophie was safe at school, you were in a safe place, and it hit you. Good timing, actually."

"Yeah." She gave a short, mirthless laugh. "There's this level I was operating at, where I was in control and focused on doing what I needed to. Then, *bam,* I lost it."

"That's okay. Now you're back in control."

She glanced at him. "I guess you know about this stuff."

"Too much about it."

Surprising herself, she took his hand, feeling its strength, size and power. It was a toughened hand, calloused and firm. She squeezed it gently. "Thanks, Ethan."

He didn't pull away. "Nothing to thank me for. There have been times when I wanted to beat my head against a wall until it hurt so bad I couldn't feel anything else. I never gave in, but I think you know what I mean."

"Yeah, I think I do."

All of a sudden she felt a whole lot better about things. She had an ally. An ally who understood. "So Micah is…your father?"

"Yeah."

"I'm sorry, but I never heard about you before."

"He didn't know about me."

"I'm so sorry."

"Can't say that I am." He shrugged. "I never knew him, so I never knew what I was missing. A few times when I was a kid I got angry at my mother for never giving us a chance, but I finally understood. She was scared."

"Scared?"

"Micah was in special ops. He'd go away suddenly, without warning, and she never knew when or if he'd come back. She couldn't handle the strain."

"I guess I can see that."

"Eventually so did I. She explained to me that she just couldn't see raising a kid that way. That *she* couldn't live that way."

"Did you have a stepfather?"

"That was the interesting thing. She'd date once in a while, but she never married. I don't know why."

They were talking about some very painful things, Connie realized, and both of them were acting as if they meant nothing. Just chatting casually about things that had at one time or another nearly cut them in two emotionally.

When she thought about her marriage, which was rare, she thought of it as being behind a glass wall. She could see it, remember it, but it no longer had the power to touch her. She wondered if Ethan had learned to do the same thing.

Unfortunately, the feelings, the pain, were still there and could escape at any time to inflict emotional mayhem.

Growing uncomfortable, she withdrew her hand from Ethan's and tried to slow her suddenly racing heart.

After a moment she said through a constricted throat, "I just realized something."

"What's that?"

"When the unthinkable has happened in your life, you live in constant fear of the worst."

He fell silent as they continued walking. They reached the corner, then continued to the right. The school was only two blocks away. ·

"Yeah," he said finally. "You do."

It was then that she noticed he wasn't looking around in the same way she was. She scanned things at street level exclusively, seeking shadows behind shrubs, people sitting in cars, danger in alleyways.

He scanned the ground level, too, but spent much less time on it. He looked higher, as well, to rooftops and upper-story windows. His perception of possible threat seemed significantly greater than hers.

But of course it would be, she realized. Nothing in her life could compare to war.

All of a sudden she felt as if she'd been whining. He'd seen things she couldn't even imagine, had probably lost friends in the ugliest ways imaginable.

But Sophie… Sophie was precious, too. Incalculably precious. To her. Ethan seemed to understand that or he wouldn't be here with her right now.

Nor had he given her any sense at all that he didn't consider her feelings and her daughter to be as important as anything he had ever dealt with.

She felt a warm flutter toward him, and a burst of gratitude. "Thanks so much for helping me with this."

"What kind of man would I be if I didn't?"

She glanced at him before returning her attention to the street. "Trust me, there are men who wouldn't."

"Well, I'm not one of them. If there's one thing I've learned, it's that every single life is precious."

She believed him. And in believing him, she understood the horror of the life he'd led. By choice or by mandate, he had sundered his soul.

They reached the school. Around it, everything was dead quiet, so they took the time to walk the perimeter. Nothing caught their attention, but by the time they reached the front of the school again, busses were pulling into the circular drive, and cars were pulling into the parking lot.

Connie looked at her watch. "Five minutes till the bell."

He nodded. "I'm going to stand back a little and watch while you collect Sophie."

She understood. Only one of them should be looking

for Sophie, the other should be keeping a lookout. "Don't stand too far away," she said. "You don't want to look suspicious yourself."

He nodded acknowledgment and stepped back only a couple of feet. In his chambray shirt and jeans, he looked pretty much like anyone else around here who was over thirty, except perhaps for the heritage writ plain on his face. He received more than one look from arriving parents, but no one approached him, perhaps because he stood in a way that indicated he was with Connie.

A group of teachers and administrators emerged from the building, smiling and saying hello to everyone, but taking no time to pause in conversation. They looked around as uneasily as anyone.

Shortly after, the bell rang over speakers inside and out. Within fifteen seconds kids began erupting through the doors, headed for buses or parents.

Sophie arrived within a couple of minutes. She ran over and threw her arms around Connie's waist, hugging her tightly but giggling at the same time.

"Jeremy has green hair!" she exclaimed.

"How did he get green hair?" Connie asked, squatting to eye level with her daughter.

"He painted it in art class. Mrs. Belgia tried to wash it out, but it stained. His mom is gonna be *sooo* mad."

"Maybe." Although if Connie knew Jeremy's mother as well as she thought, she figured the woman was going to laugh herself silly. Far better than getting angry, in her experience. And Jeremy would have to live with the hair.

Connie stroked her daughter's blond curls. "I'm glad you didn't decide to paint yours. I like it the way it is."

"Me, too." Sophie beamed.

Connie straightened, taking her daughter's hand. "I want you to meet a friend of mine. He's going to be staying with us for a little while. Ethan, this is my daughter, Sophie. Sophie, this is Mr. Ethan."

Sophie looked up, then up farther, her eyes widening. "You're an Indian!" she blurted.

For an instant Connie wished she could stuff cotton in Sophie's mouth.

But Ethan only smiled and squatted, the soccer ball still under his arm. "I am," he said. "You've seen Indians before, right?"

"Yeah." Sophie grinned. "I think they're cool. I wish I was Pocohantas."

"Like in the movie?"

"Yeah. She's beautiful."

"Not as beautiful as you."

Sophie's brow creased. "Why not?"

"Cuz she's not seven years old, plus she's only a cartoon."

Sophie giggled. "I *know* that. What's the ball for?"

"I thought we could kick it around a little at the park."

"Cool." Sophie tugged her mother's hand. "Let's go."

With Sophie skipping and holding her hand, Connie started walking toward the park. Ethan was on her other side.

Part of her felt relieved that Sophie didn't seem afraid, but another part worried about Sophie's ready acceptance of Ethan. Of course, she'd introduced him to Sophie herself, but still…

"Maybe," she said quietly as Sophie sang cheerfully about the wheels on the bus as they passed the long line of waiting vehicles, "a little shyness would do her some good."

"Naw," said Ethan, just as quietly. "I didn't mind what she said, and you don't want to change her because of this thing."

"No." She looked at him. "That really worries me. That this *could* change her."

"Then don't let it."

"Easier said than done, I fear."

Sophie waved to friends, skipping along tirelessly, eager to get to the park. Connie kept scanning for anything the least bit suspicious but saw nothing. Everyone who was there should have been there. Nobody lurked or seemed out of place.

And the farther they got from the school, the thinner the crowds became, until they were nearly by themselves.

"Where's Jody?" Connie asked Sophie. "I didn't see her. I thought the two of you were stuck together like bubblegum."

Sophie giggled again and downshifted from skip to walk. "She didn't come to school today. I think maybe she was sick."

Connie's heart slammed. "I'll call and check on her."

What if something had happened to Jody? But then she reminded herself that Jody's mother had been the first to learn of what had happened, apart from the police. So maybe she had just kept Jody at home today.

"I got a surprise for you," she told Sophie.

"Yeah? What?"

"A cell phone."

"Oh, boy!" Sophie let out a shriek of delight. "I get my own cell phone!"

"I got one for me, too, so when we get home, we'll figure out how to work them, and then I'm going to give you some rules."

Sophie's face scrunched up. "Everything has rules."

"Everything," Connie agreed.

Sophie peered around at Ethan. "Do you have rules, too?"

"Lots of them," he said. "More than you do, I bet."

"How come?"

"Because I was a soldier."

"Oh."

"Lots of rules for soldiers."

Sophie shook her head. "Not as many as my mom makes."

Ethan laughed. "We'll see about that."

They reached the park without seeing anything unusual, which contradictorily both eased Connie's mind and heightened her fear. No threat right now, but what if the threat was merely hiding and waiting?

She shook her head, trying to clear it of such thoughts. No good to think that way. Utterly useless worrying.

No one else was at the park. Not a single swing moved. Connie would have expected to see at least a few children, preschoolers out with their mothers, if nothing else. Cold winters made spring days welcome and cherished, but apparently everyone had hunkered down.

Ethan chose an open patch of ground between the swings and the baseball diamond, and set the ball down. "We're just going to practice kicking it around, okay? Because there's no one else here yet to play with."

Sophie nodded and dropped her backpack on the ground. "Everyone's scared because of that man yesterday."

"Are you scared?"

"A little. But I'm not alone."

"Right." Ethan smiled. "Have you ever kicked a soccer ball before?"

"Once in gym class. I wasn't very good."

"Then we'll work on making you the best kicker in your class."

Sophie nodded. "Yeah. The best."

"That's what we'll shoot for."

Connie stepped back, giving them room and pretending to absently look around, although there was nothing absentminded in her surveillance of the area.

She listened while Ethan showed Sophie how to kick with the side of her foot, not her toe. Pretty soon she got the hang of it and was kicking the ball where she wanted it to go. Both Connie and Ethan applauded her efforts.

A few minutes later, Sophie and Ethan were kicking the ball back and forth, even running with it a bit, every move accompanied by Sophie's cries of delight.

Connie would have bet Ethan hadn't a thought to spare for anything except the little game he and Sophie were playing. But then, in one dreadful moment, she learned otherwise.

"Let's go," Ethan said. His tone was level. Connie's gaze snapped to his face. He was looking at something behind her. Instinctively she whirled around, but she saw nothing.

"I don't wanna go," Sophie argued. "This is fun."

"We'll play more later," Ethan said. "Connie, take Sophie home. She needs a drink of water."

"But—"

Connie took her daughter's hand. "Let's go, sweetie." She hoped her voice didn't betray the sudden terror and tension she was feeling. "We've got cell phones to learn how to use, remember?"

Apparently that didn't seem important, because Sophie continued to pout as she left with her mother.

Ethan dashed away, soccer ball abandoned on the field.

Chapter 7

Connie paced, trying to ease the tension in every muscle of her body. Julia kept telling her daughter to calm down and have some coffee, but Connie hardly heard her. All she could think of was the way Ethan had looked—and the way he had suddenly run off.

He'd seen something. Someone had been watching them, she was sure of it. For the hundredth time, she went upstairs and checked on Sophie, who was already in command of her cell phone and calling friends on it.

"Jody's mom didn't have the car today," she told Connie on one of her trips through the house.

"I know. I called."

"Okay."

"How'd you figure out how to use the phone so fast?"

Sophie rolled her eyes. "It's *easy,* Mom."

"I guess you'll have to show me."

"Sure."

"Later."

"Okay." Sophie went back to her giggling conversation with Jody. At least Connie presumed it was Jody.

Connie walked around the house yet again, looking out all the windows, then went back downstairs, checking the perimeter from inside.

"You're going to drive me crazy, girl," Julia said. "Sit."

This time Connie obeyed, even though her entire body felt electrified with the urge to move.

"You don't know that he saw a threat," Julia reminded her. "Remember, he doesn't know folks around here. He could be mistaken."

"Yeah. Of course."

Julia pushed a cup of coffee over to her. "Now listen to me, Connie. You'll be of no earthly use to anyone if you wear yourself out over nothing. Which is exactly what you're doing."

Connie snapped. "Don't you get it, Mom? Some stranger knows Sophie's *name.*"

"I get it, all right. I also get that everyone in this county is on high alert right now, and if some stranger approaches *any* child, he's apt to be shot before he's questioned."

It was true, Connie knew. Maybe not the shooting

part, but nobody around here was going to turn a blind eye to anything now. Not anything.

"Your neighbors are watching out for Sophie. For all the kids," Julia said. "You know that."

Connie drew a deep breath and tried to release some of the tension. "You're right," she said.

"Of course I'm right. I'm always right."

Connie managed a wan smile. "Very true."

Julia patted her hand. "Just hang in there. If the guy isn't gone, he'll get caught. In the meantime, everything possible is being done."

Also true.

But it still wasn't *enough*.

Just then, just as Connie was struggling with a desire to crawl out of her own skin as she tried to sit calmly at the table, Ethan entered through the kitchen door.

"Wild-goose chase," he said succinctly.

"What did you see?"

"I thought I saw someone lurking in the bushes. If he was there, I sure as hell couldn't find any evidence of it. Sorry I scared you."

"Sit down," Julia said, "and have some coffee with us. Thank you for trying to protect Sophie."

Thank you? Connie thought. *Thank you for scaring me out of my wits,* she wanted to scream. But she knew that wasn't fair even as she thought it, so she bit the words back. Instead, she filled her mouth with bitter coffee.

"How's Sophie?" Ethan asked. He poured his own coffee and joined them.

"Oh, Sophie," Connie said, trying not to let the tension seep into her words. "She's so excited about having a cell phone, I doubt she noticed anything."

"Good." He sat across from her, studying her from dark eyes that seemed to see through her. The feeling was discomfiting, and she wanted to look away, but she couldn't. "At least there's one person I didn't scare."

Connie bit her lip, guilt edging into anger's place. "Sorry," she said. "I've been worried to death."

"Of course," he answered. "You can yell at me if you want."

His words acted like a pin, puncturing the last of her tension. A sigh escaped her as she rested her forehead on her hand. "You didn't find anything at all?"

"No."

The word hung on the air, bald and uncompromising, but its very brevity seemed to say something. Connie lifted her head. "There *was* someone there."

His face took on that carved look again, as if it had turned to stone.

"What did you find?" she demanded.

"Nothing." He shook his head. "I don't usually hallucinate. My life depends on seeing what's really there. I thought I saw something. I don't like being wrong."

That was a whole mouthful, Connie thought. A butterfly returned to her stomach.

Julia apparently missed the subtext, however, because she said kindly, "We all make mistakes, Ethan. God never made a perfect man or woman."

"No," he agreed. "Thank God."

* * *

Later, much later, after Julia and Sophie had gone to bed and to sleep, Connie found Ethan sitting up in the darkened living room. He hadn't even spread out the blankets and sheets she'd given him earlier.

"Are you going to stay up all night?" she asked. "You need some sleep."

"You're one to talk." He turned in the darkness, and she caught the glimmer of his eyes. In the faint misty light that came through the sheer curtains, he became a figure of myth, a tall man with long hair, lacking only a shield and a sword to complete the image. Deep down inside, sensations began to stir, sensations she had banished to hell years ago.

Instinctively, she pulled her robe tighter and held it closed over her breasts.

"I can sleep while Sophie's in school tomorrow," he said. Apparently he sensed the awkwardness in the silence, too.

"Coffee?" she asked. "I thought it was just going to be me, so I planned on making tea, but since you're a night owl, too, we might as well make coffee."

"That would be great."

Much to her relief, he didn't follow. She made the coffee in the dark, waiting patiently for it to perk, thinking it was high time she got a drip coffeemaker. In short, anything that didn't involve thinking about Sophie and the threat.

Or the man in her living room.

Some kind of preternatural shiver passed through

her, focusing her mind on how Ethan had looked standing in the dark. Some psychic part of her clamored that she had business with him, though she couldn't imagine what.

Oh, hell, yes she could. It didn't take that big a leap to realize he drew her in some elemental way. Worrying about Sophie had kept her from recognizing other feelings, but here in the dark, they surged to the surface.

She could have turned on the lights, but she didn't. She didn't want to rupture the spell. It provided a much needed distraction right now, this yearning and need. This aching hunger that had grown unseen until it sprang from the jungle of her subconscious.

He would be safe, she realized. He would go away and take all the complications with him.

At once shock filled her. She didn't think that way. She had never thought that way.

The aroma of the coffee filled her nostrils, speaking of hot, delightful, yet bitter flavors. Turning, she switched off the flame beneath the burner and filled two mugs. Strong and black.

Ethan still stood in the living room, looking out through the sheers at the street. She went to stand beside him and passed him a mug when he glanced at her.

"Thanks," he said.

She didn't reply. The spell locked her voice in her throat. An aura surrounded him. Holding her mug in both hands, closing her eyes, she sensed an emanation of power, strength and something far greater. For a moment she knew with certainty that if she opened her eyes, she would see him surrounded by rainbows. Crazy.

He spoke, his voice like night, all black velvet. "My people," he said slowly, "believe that everything is alive, even the rocks."

"Yes?"

"Yes. My mother was Cheyenne. She taught me some of the old ways and had her brother give me some training in what I suppose could be called the occult."

She faced him then, forgetting everything else. "Shamanic tradition?"

"Yes."

"Wow." She barely breathed the word.

"Of course, it didn't fit with most of what I was learning elsewhere or with my friends, so I took it all with a large grain of salt."

"But now?"

"But now…" He shook his head. "I've felt the rocks cry out in protest at the blood spilled on them. I have heard the thunder speak. The ways of my mother's people are as valid as your ways."

Connie nodded. He *did* have an aura, she thought. She couldn't see it, but she sure as hell could feel it, humming around him.

Almost in answer to what he had just said, a crack of thunder rent the night.

Connie bit her lip, waiting. The air around them crackled.

"I'll protect your daughter," he said. "But know this."

She waited, her heart freezing.

"The danger is still there. I sense it. And it's closing in."

She wanted to scream at him that he was just trying to scare her, but deep in her very soul his words resonated with truth.

"Are you psychic?" she asked finally.

"Not really. If I were, many of my friends would still be walking this earth. But I *am* a mystic. I will admit that."

"And you sense things."

He looked at her, his eyes glimmering. "I sense things."

Turning, she put her coffee on an end table and wrapped her arms tightly around herself. "I can't stand this."

He astonished her, opening his arms and drawing her close, holding her snugly and comfortingly. Her head rested on his hard chest, and she could hear his heartbeat, a steady thud.

Tension, a tight spring inside her, began to loosen, as if his touch held soothing magic. His embrace seemed like a safe haven, an experience she had never known.

Then his fingers found their way into her hair, stroking and massaging gently.

He didn't offer any false promises, merely the sense that she wouldn't be alone. A ridiculous feeling, when the whole county shared her concern. But this felt closer and more intimate, more real.

They stood together for a long time, coffee forgotten, everything forgotten. Another crack of thunder, this one even louder, drove them apart.

Connie jumped back. Then, embarrassed, she reached for her coffee and retreated to an armchair. He, too, picked up his mug, then turned to face the window again, watching the flickers of lightning brighten the night.

Eventually she found her voice again. "What do you mean when you say you've heard the thunder speak?"

He turned slightly in her direction. "Just that. If you listen, it can speak to you. Not that I'm going to say it happens all the time. You're a Christian, right?"

"Yes."

"Have you ever heard God's voice in your heart?"

"A few times."

"Well, it's the same. Sometimes I hear the thunder in my heart. It speaks to me."

"And the stones?"

"The stones are alive. Everything is alive, Connie. That's where we make our biggest mistake, I think, believing that some things aren't. Or maybe a better word would be *aware*. Everything is aware. That's why my uncle taught me to give thanks for even the smallest things. Give thanks to the tree before you cut it, things like that."

"I happen to think that's a beautiful way of looking at the world."

"It could be."

He returned his attention to the street. Lightning

flashed brightly again, followed by a boom of thunder. "Give thanks to the rain, to the food you eat. To the mountains that shelter you. It's not exactly pantheistic, at least not the way my uncle taught me. But it does recognize the importance of everything in our world."

Intuition made her say, "You haven't thought about this for a long time, have you."

Another flicker of lightning limned his figure against the curtains, and she saw echoes of ancient warriors in the afterimage.

"No, I haven't. For years now, I haven't really had time to think about that part of myself except in a general way. I've been too focused on external reality. On trying to survive and keep my fellows alive. Not much room for anything else."

"I wouldn't think so. But now you have time."

"I do." He bent, retrieving his mug and sipping. "You make great coffee."

"Thanks."

The voice of thunder spoke again, a deep rolling rumble. Yet no rain fell.

"What I saw earlier today…" He hesitated.

"Go on. At this point I would believe you if you told me that you saw a leprechaun all dressed in green."

A chuckle escaped him, a sound not unlike the thunder. "No leprechauns. Something else."

She leaned forward, resting her elbows on her knees. "Tell me."

"What I saw wasn't there. It wasn't a man. But I didn't hallucinate, either."

"Meaning?"

"I didn't see with the eyes in my head."

Shock slammed her chest like a semi running out of control. She couldn't breathe; no air remained in the room. Finally, sucking in something that posed as air, she managed to say, "I don't understand. Why did you run after it if it wasn't real?"

"It *was* real," he said with certainty. "I hoped to learn more, but I failed. All I can tell you is that the threat has not gone."

"He's still here?"

"And looking for your daughter."

That put paid to any possibility of sleep for Connie. She drained her coffee mug, then went to refill it. When she returned to the living room, Ethan was sitting on the couch, holding his own mug. He was turned to the side so he could continue to look out the front window.

Lightning flashed, thunder boomed hollowly, and the fury seemed to be trying creep indoors.

Connie spoke. "You can't know that."

"Perhaps not."

He didn't seem to mean it, and she didn't believe him, anyway. She considered herself a practical, prosaic person, but she also knew that was a bit of self-delusion. She'd had premonitions in her life. She'd had moments of absolute knowing that couldn't be explained any other way. Not many, but enough to give her respect for Ethan's intuition.

"Sorry," she said after a moment. Her hand shook

so badly she put her coffee down. "I'm trying to find denial here."

He nodded. "I can understand that. But even if you do manage it, you won't stay in denial long. You're not the type."

"Maybe not anymore. I used to be pretty good at it."

"During your marriage."

"Yes."

That time the lightning flash blinded her, washing out the room with its glare. Then a crack of thunder threatened to rend the world. A cry from upstairs brought Connie from her chair and toward the stairway as if springs had ejected her.

Even so, Ethan beat her to it. He reached the top of the stairs when she was still only two-thirds of the way up.

She heard the bedroom door open, saw the light spill on as he flipped the switch. A couple of seconds later she was looking into her daughter's bedroom. Sophie, pale-faced, was sitting upright in bed. "I'm scared," she said.

Connie moved toward her. "That was sure loud, honey," she agreed. She sat on the edge of her daughter's bed and pulled the girl into a hug. "It made me jump, too."

"I wanna come downstairs."

"Fair enough," Connie agreed. "Hot milk?"

"Hot chocolate."

"Hmmm." Connie pretended to think about it, hoping Sophie couldn't hear how hard her heart was hammering. "Well, okay…"

A wan smile formed on Sophie's mouth, but her eyes remained pinched.

It was too much for her, Connie thought. First the attempted abduction, and now this storm. *Straw, camel, back,* she thought. "Okay, let's go downstairs. Hot chocolate sounds wonderful."

Another crack of thunder shook the house to its foundations. Sophie looked up, clearly trying to be brave. "This is a nasty storm."

"It sure is. Bad, bad, bad storm," Connie added, as if scolding the weather.

Sophie's smile grew more natural. Connie helped her daughter into her slippers and robe, and took her hand so they could walk down to the kitchen together.

Only as they moved toward the door did she realize that Ethan had vanished.

Gone like a ghost.

In the kitchen, with the lights all on, Connie began to warm milk. The storm had reached a peak of rage, shooting bullets of rain at the windows. Every growl of thunder made the house tremble. Long before the milk began to simmer, Julia appeared in her wheelchair.

"Goodness!" she said. "Only the dead could sleep through this."

"Maybe they're not," Connie remarked.

"Yeah," Sophie said. "Maybe they're sitting on their tombstones and wishing it would quiet down."

Julia and Connie both laughed.

"Where's Deputy Ethan?" Sophie asked.

"I don't know," Connie answered truthfully. "Mom, will you watch the milk while I get him?"

"As if you need to ask."

Connie didn't exactly want Ethan to join the family circle; he'd already breached too many of her defensive barriers, leaving her exposed. But if it made Sophie feel more secure…

He had returned to the living room, to his guardian position.

"Sophie wants you to join us," she said.

"Not necessary," he replied quietly.

"I didn't say it was. You've been invited."

She clearly saw him hesitate in the glare of another lightning flash from outside, but then he turned to follow her. "Thank you," he said.

The kitchen, the heart of this family, which ordinarily welcomed her with warmth, felt odd tonight. Alien. And it wasn't Ethan who made it feel that way. It was something about the storm, Connie thought. Something had leached away the comfort she usually found here.

As they drank, Sophie announced, "I don't want to go to school tomorrow."

Connie hesitated. Part of her wanted to wrap Sophie up and keep her right here beside her until the threat vanished, but another part of her of understood that would be a bad way to handle the situation. It would teach Sophie all the wrong lessons about dealing with fear.

Her hesitation gave Julia time to enter the breach. "Don't you feel well, dear?"

Sophie shook her head. "My stomach hurts."

Another boom of thunder caused the table to shake and their mugs to slide a bit. *Wisdom,* Connie thought. *Grant me wisdom. How do I deal with this?*

Julia knew no such qualms. "We'll see how you feel in the morning."

Ethan spoke. "It's all right to be afraid, Sophie."

"Do you get afraid?"

"All the time. I used to be a soldier. I was afraid every day."

"What did you do?"

"I did my job, anyway."

Sophie nodded, her young face serious. Maybe too serious. "That's what you're supposed to do," she agreed. "Mom says fear is like a warning signal, and all it means is to be careful and think first."

"That's very wise," Ethan agreed.

"But my stomach still hurts. I wanna puke."

"Then don't drink that chocolate, child," Julia said. "Heavens, that's the worst thing when you feel that way. Let me get you a little ginger ale."

Sophie screwed up her face. "No. I don't want anything."

Watching her daughter, listening to her, Connie felt capable of murder. If she ever got her hands on the man who had frightened Sophie, he might never see the light of another day. Her hands gripped her mug so tightly her knuckles turned white.

She looked from Sophie to Ethan and saw a wealth of understanding in his dark gaze.

"Tell you what," Julia said. "You can sleep in my bed

with me. It's close to the bathroom, in case you get sick."

"I *am* sick," Sophie said. She shivered. Then she leaped up from her chair and ran to the bathroom. Connie followed to find her daughter being sick in the toilet.

She grabbed a washcloth, wet it with cold water and pressed it to the back of her daughter's neck, speaking soothing words about nothing, rubbing Sophie's back until the dry heaves stopped.

When Sophie at last caught her breath and straightened, she looked white as a ghost.

"Well, that settles it," Connie said as she gently wiped her daughter's face, then helped her rinse her mouth. "You're staying home tomorrow."

"I *said* I was sick."

"So you did. And you certainly proved it."

Sophie looked grumpy. "You just thought I was scared, like a little kid."

"Sometimes it happens."

"But I don't wanna sleep upstairs until the storm is gone."

"No, of course not. This is the worst storm I can remember in a long time. I don't want to sleep upstairs, either."

"I'll sleep with Grandma."

So it was settled. A little while later, Julia and Sophie were tucked into Julia's bed, with a light on. Connie went back to the kitchen and found that Ethan had once again disappeared. The man had a way of doing that.

She made more coffee and poured herself a cup, listening to the storm, wondering if they might get a tornado. It sounded violent enough.

Then, as if drawn by an invisible wire, she returned to the living room.

Ethan was still there, standing at his chosen post. Connie sank into the armchair. "I don't think this is fair to you."

He turned to look at her. "Why not?"

"Well, you came here to see your father, and instead, you're living in my house, protecting my daughter, and your father's at the other end of the county."

He sat facing her, stretching his legs out before him. "It's good to be useful. As for Micah and me…we have no history to speak of. There's a silence between us. It may take years to cross it."

"But you can hardly do that while you're stuck here."

"Do you want me to go?"

Part of her did, but most of her didn't. "No. No. That's not what I meant. What kind of silence are you talking about?"

"It's hard to explain."

"So many things are."

"They seem to be," he agreed. In another flash of light from outside, she saw him rub his bearded chin. "There's a time," he said, "when silence speaks best. A time when just being with someone gradually creates a knowing. This is one of those times. He only just learned about me, and I never knew anything about him at all, really. It's not as if we can simply sit down and share the last thirty-some years in a burst of words."

"I can understand that." But she thought how odd it must be. It would be like that for Sophie, she realized, if that son of a gun ever returned. She prayed every night he never would, because with hindsight she could see that he'd never had a thing to recommend him, and she certainly had no reason to think he'd changed. "Has it been hard?" The devil made her ask as she thought of her daughter.

"Not knowing him? Not really. I understood why my mother chose as she did, and I respect that. There were a few times when I felt a little resentful that I didn't have a father the way other kids did. But not often."

Connie sighed. "Sometimes I worry about that with Sophie."

"You couldn't have raised her with that man."

"Absolutely not! But how old will she have to be to understand that?"

"Maybe not very old at all. Like I said, *I* understood, and my mother's reasons were very different from yours. Micah never abused her. She just didn't want to live the lifestyle. Her choice was purely selfish, and yet I understood it."

Connie tipped her head to one side. "Are you so sure it was purely selfish? Maybe she was thinking about trying to raise a child in those circumstances."

"It wouldn't have been easy," he agreed. "But I don't think she really loved him, either. It was, as the song says, just one of those things."

"Perhaps. You're very philosophical about it."

"I've had time to think."

She nodded and transferred her gaze to the window as the wind took a sudden turn at battering the house. "This is going to go on all night."

"Seems like."

"So everything went well when you met Micah?" she asked, quickly changing tack.

"Better than I expected. Faith wanted me to move in."

At that, Connie chuckled. "She'd mother the whole world if she could. They make a truly interesting pair."

"What do you mean?"

"Well, you wouldn't ordinarily think of the two of them together, they're so different in so many ways. Yet she seems to touch a place in him, and he in her, that welds them. When they're together, you feel the sense of magic."

"I noticed that." He crossed his legs at the ankle. "Some families seem to make a circle around themselves, like a spell. They have that."

Connie nodded. "Exactly."

"So do you, with Sophie and your mother."

Connie smiled. "Thanks. I like to think so."

"I can feel it. It's good." He rose without warning and went to the window. He didn't speak, and Connie found herself holding her breath, waiting. The rain had stopped, but the wind still rushed.

"I'm going outside," he said.

"Why?"

"I just want to walk around the house."

"God, you're creeping me out! Did you see some-thing?"

"No. No. It's just my training."

"What training?"

"A storm is good cover for an approach. It doesn't mean anything except that I won't be able to relax until I check."

She watched him stride out, thinking that his life had marked him deeply. Very deeply.

Most people carried scars from the past, but his wounds remained deep and fresh.

Would he ever let down his guard?

Chapter 8

Over the next several days, life began to return to normal. Children again played in the park after school, the school itself resumed regular recesses, and while kids still walked in groups, as advised, parents no longer hovered over them every instant.

Even the police presence seemed to have lightened, although Connie knew that was far from true. Most everyone else assumed the creep had moved on. Not Connie. That creep had known her daughter's name.

Even so, she had to allow Sophie to return to some semblance of normalcy, walking home with her friends again, laughing and playing. She couldn't keep her daughter under constant lock and key.

But she remained watchful, and she was sure

Ethan did, as well, even though he sometimes appeared to be invisible.

For her part, Gage assigned her to an in-town beat during the days, which meant she was available for Sophie at any time. Ordinarily she disliked working in town, preferring to cover the county's wide-open spaces and deal with the ranchers' families. Working in town usually bored her.

Not right now.

Her third day on the shift, Micah Parish shared the car with her. She wondered what Gage had been thinking, if there was some particular reason.

Apparently so. Micah, usually a quiet man, opened a conversation several hours into the shift. "How's it going with Ethan?"

"Fine," she admitted. "He's not a problem, if that's what you mean."

"Not exactly."

"Oh." She waited, knowing from experience that pressing Micah often led directly to a stone wall.

"I was just wondering what you think of him."

"He seems like a pretty nice guy. For some odd reason he reminds me of you."

Micah laughed. "Faith said exactly the same thing."

"You're not getting much of a chance to know him."

"That'll come."

Connie hesitated. "It must have been a shock when he showed up."

"Not exactly. Somehow, at some level, I almost expected it."

"As if you knew?"

"As if I knew."

"Maybe you should come over to my place after school gets out. You could spend some time with him."

"He's not ready yet."

She glanced at Micah, then took the risk. "How can you know that?"

She expected the stone wall of silence, but he surprised her. "I just do. He knows where to find me."

Connie managed to stifle a sigh of exasperation. Ethan had come all this way, to the virtual middle of nowhere, to find his father, and now he wasn't ready to talk to the man? Why did she find that so hard to believe?

Yet Ethan had said much the same thing. Something about needing the silence first.

She was still thinking about that near shift's end, and she positioned herself strategically to keep an eye out for Sophie as she pulled up near the school and Micah got out. He walked up the street, as if checking the cars parked along the curb.

Even with the cover of routine patrol and Micah checking cars for parking violations, he was still too visible, Connie thought. Still too visible to someone trying to avoid them. This wasn't exactly the porous surveillance Nathan had recommended. Yet how far could she let the risk run?

Life was all about risk. She knew that. Complete safety existed only in a padded cell, and perhaps not even there. But while she could risk herself, she found it impossible to risk her daughter.

She scanned the street again and noted that Micah had vanished from sight. Like father, like son. Ghost men.

She let out the brake and resumed cruising, circling the general area where the kids would walk as they left school, but trying not to get too close. Micah was surely out there somewhere, watching, as was Ethan. She could afford to create the appearance of space.

She stopped at one point to put a warning on a car with a broken taillight. She waved to the crossing guards who began to appear on corners. She knew every one of them as a neighbor. That was the wonderful thing about Conard County. Even with the recent growth, she could still get to know nearly everyone.

It was also the reason she had always felt safe here. But all of that now lay shattered like a broken mirror, reflecting scattered, distorted images.

Had it ever been safe here? Or was that an illusion?

She watched the schoolchildren as they scattered toward their homes. As usual, she enjoyed watching them and their sheer exuberance. It reminded her of the days when getting out of school for the afternoon had been enough to fill her with elation.

Unfortunately, it seemed to take a lot more to excite her these days. It occurred to her that the human race would probably be a lot healthier if they could hang on to some of that joy, wonder and exuberance later in life.

Or maybe that was just a lousy perspective to take. Maybe adults crushed themselves.

Then, once again, her thoughts wandered to Ethan. They kept doing that. Her mind, she thought wryly, had a mind of its own. Here she was, prowling the streets looking for a potential criminal, and she was thinking of Ethan.

And her thoughts, heaven help her, reeked of sexual attraction and desire. Funny thing, that. It always sprang up when you least wanted it. And, as she'd learned, often for the wrong person. After her ex, she just plain didn't trust her judgment of men that way. Now Ethan, a man she hardly knew, was turning the key in the locked box of her desires.

She'd tested the secure power of his arms, the hard muscles of his chest, in that single comforting embrace. But she hadn't felt his skin, and she found herself wanting to know in the worst way what his skin felt like. Warm and smooth? Rough?

Damn!

At that moment, she spied Sophie coming around a corner from an unexpected direction. Worse, she was alone.

Connie's heart accelerated along with her patrol car as she zoomed over to her daughter. Sophie looked over and smiled.

"Hi, Mom."

"Where are Jody and your other friends?"

Sophie shrugged. "I dunno."

"Climb in and I'll take you home."

Sophie did as she was told, climbing into the passenger seat, sitting with her book bag on her lap.

"Sweetie, you know you're not supposed to walk home alone."

"I guess I missed the others."

"How come?"

"I dunno."

When she paused at a stop sign, Connie looked over at Sophie. "What aren't you telling me?"

Sophie's lower lip stuck out. "Nothing."

For the first time in a long time, Connie didn't believe her daughter. "Honey, you know there's nothing that makes me madder than a lie."

"I'm not lying!"

"Okay." Connie thought about that, admitting that *I dunno* was the kids' equivalent of *I don't recall* under oath. "You're going to be a great lawyer someday."

Sophie looked at her. "Huh?"

"Never mind. Look, there's Micah. I need to stop for him, because we're supposed to be working together today."

"Okay."

Micah stood on the sidewalk, watching her approach, and when she pulled up and rolled down her window, he bent to look in. "I see you found Little Miss Lost."

"Lost?" Connie turned her head to look at Sophie. "Sophie, where did you go?"

"Nowhere," Sophie said. "I told you. I dunno where the other kids went."

Connie looked at Micah. "Later," he said. "Take her on home. Ethan and I are going to stop for a coffee and a chat. Gage said for you to take the rest of the day."

Connie nodded, her teeth clenched, sure Micah

wasn't telling her everything. One certainty leaped out at her, however: Gage hadn't told them to take the rest of the day over nothing.

"Later," Micah said again. "Ethan and I will be over shortly, if you don't mind."

"I'll put the coffee on."

"Thanks."

She met Micah's obsidian gaze and saw reassurance there. Forcing herself to relax, she lifted her foot from the brake and drove toward her house.

Ethan and Micah met at Maude's diner. Midafternoon, the place was quiet, with only Maude about to handle things. She poured their coffee, then disappeared into the back. The banging that carried through the kitchen door indicated that she might be involved in dinner preparation.

The two men, so alike yet so different, looked at one another across the table. The words, it seemed, still weren't there.

Finally Ethan broke the silence. "This thing with Sophie Halloran… I don't like it."

"Me, neither." Micah sipped his coffee. "Connie tell you about her marriage?"

"A bit. As if it were the distant past."

Micah nodded. "Faith went through something similar. When I met her, she was running from her husband, and a couple of weeks after she got here, he found her and tried to kill her."

Ethan's eyes narrowed. "And?"

Micah shrugged. "I was a deputy. I got there in time. He's gone."

Ethan nodded, as if approving. "Are you suggesting that Connie might be facing the same threat?"

"Not directly." Micah looked down at his mug and suddenly smiled. "You'll never know how many of the problems of life Faith and I solved over a cup of coffee."

Ethan answered with a similar smile. "Good time to talk."

"Especially when winter is howling outside. But back to Connie. She talks like it's all in the past and she's long over it. But I can tell you from my experience with Faith, she's *not* over it. She's buried it. That woman hasn't dated in all the time she's been here. Tells you something, because there are plenty of men around here who have asked."

Ethan nodded. "I got the feeling her rendition was more cover than fact."

"It is. When we did her background check before hiring her, I discovered the story was a lot uglier than the way she tells it. She sort of does the outline thing, like she's reading from a list of all the abused-spouse indicators. It doesn't get personal. But trust me, Ethan, it was personal. Very personal and very ugly."

"Kid gloves, then."

"That would be my advice." Micah leaned back and sighed heavily.

"You think this has something to do with Sophie?"

"It might. You know what evil men are capable of.

You don't need me to draw you a picture. They say hell hath no fury like a woman scorned, but I can tell you, men are worse. Far worse. And if this guy is still p.o.'d that Connie got away, there's no telling what he might do to get even."

"But why wait seven years?"

"Didn't she tell you?"

"Tell me what?"

"He went to prison for what he did. And the judge really slammed him, because she was a police officer."

Ethan lowered his head a moment. "When did he get out?"

"About seven months ago."

"Does Connie know that?"

"I don't know. Probably. We got a routine notice through the office, because she lives here now."

"She never mentioned it. She doesn't even seem worried about that."

"Then maybe she *doesn't* know. Or maybe she thinks she covered her tracks well enough. She changed her last name, for one thing, after she got here. The post office has long since stopped making forwarding addresses available to the general public because of the danger. It may not have entered her head that after all this time he might come after her."

"And maybe he hasn't."

Micah nodded. "Maybe he hasn't. But I'll tell you, Ethan, I don't like that this guy knew Sophie's name. And I don't like that she disappeared today."

"Just briefly."

"Briefly is too long, under the circumstances."

Ethan sipped his coffee, thinking, reordering the pieces of the puzzle he'd been working with. "Okay. That helps."

"Maybe." Micah straightened and sipped his own coffee. "So tell me."

"Tell you what?"

"Where you've been and what you've been doing."

The question couldn't have been unexpected. Indeed, it wasn't. But Ethan had learned to compartmentalize his life in units he could handle. After a minute or so, he replied, "I think you know."

Micah waited, then nodded. "I guess I do. The hard part is figuring out how to forgive yourself."

Those words struck a chord in Ethan, seeming to crystallize a whole bunch of emotional and mental baggage. "Yeah. Have you?"

"There comes a point," Micah said slowly, "where you realize that the past is past. I'm not saying all of it was right, or even that any of it was right—or, for that matter, wrong—but it's the past, and you can't change it. So what you do, what you *have* to do, is understand that all that matters now is how you live today. If you're looking for atonement, that's the only kind you'll find. And the only way to get rid of nightmares is to build new dreams." Then he said, "I'm glad you came looking for me, son."

At that, Ethan smiled. "So am I."

Chapter 9

It was Friday evening, so one of Julia's friends picked her up for their usual "girls' night." Julia and her friends would dine at one or another's house, then go to a movie or play cards. Connie found it hard now to believe that once she had worried that her mother's confinement to a wheelchair would turn her into a shut-in.

Ethan and Micah made their appearance rather later than she expected. Sophie and she had already dined, and Sophie had vanished into her room with her cell phone. The ticker in Connie's head was already making her wonder if she'd bought enough minutes on her cell plan.

But all that faded to insignificance when the two men arrived.

"Sorry we're late," Micah said. "We went to do a little nosing around."

"Did you find anything?

"Unfortunately, no."

They gravitated to the kitchen table with their coffee, as far out of Sophie's hearing as they could get.

Connie, her nerves already shredded by Sophie's behavior after school, asked, "What did you mean by 'Little Miss Lost'?"

The men exchanged glances.

"I lost sight of her," Ethan said. "I was watching the kids come out of school, waiting for her. She came out with her friends. I moved farther down the street, trying not to be too obvious, and the next thing I knew, she wasn't there."

Connie bit out a word she rarely used.

"Exactly," said Ethan. "So I started looking. I found Micah, and we fanned out. She couldn't have been out of sight more than a minute or two, Connie. Honestly. Then I saw her walking alone along a different street toward home. I followed at a distance until she ran into you."

Connie nodded, aware that she was about to begin shaking. "She lied to me. She said she didn't know where her friends went."

"A kid's lie," Micah said. "Whatever happened in those couple of minutes, she probably did lose sight of her friends. You know, it might be nothing at all. She might have chased a squirrel, seen a dog." He shook his head. "It's obvious nothing happened to her."

"Except she's not telling me something."

"Maybe she's embarrassed because she didn't follow instructions, even scared because she lost sight of her friends."

Connie put her face in her hands, weary, worried and unsure. "I wish I could believe that."

A hand settled on her shoulder. Ethan's. The touch zapped her like electricity, almost painful in its intensity. Then the hand lifted, and she was once again alone in her own miserable little universe.

She raised her head, looking at them. "I'll make sure she doesn't do this again. Thank God it's the weekend."

Micah spoke. "Raising kids is the hardest thing I've ever done. Somehow you have to protect them without being overprotective. You need to warn them about dangers without making them scared of their own shadows. Connie, Sophie was just being a kid. They feel safer than they probably should, but you shouldn't want to take that away from them."

"I don't want to. It's just that…a few days ago she came through that door terrified because some stranger had tried to talk to her and called her by name. And then today…"

"Today the threat is in the past," Ethan said.

"Yeah," Micah agreed. "Eons ago in her mind. A week is a long time when you're seven. The whole world changes. So maybe what she did today was just some healthy hijinks. Kicking up the traces a bit. The point is, she's okay, and we'll watch more closely."

Connie nodded and managed a smile. "Sorry, guys. I'm not usually such a mess."

"You're not usually worried about your daughter." Micah stood, stretching a bit. "I need to get back to my family. You'll be okay with Ethan, Connie."

"I know."

Micah smiled. "Even bad things can sometimes bring about good."

And with that enigmatic statement, he walked out of the house.

Connie looked at Ethan. "Would you mind moving to the living room? I can hear Sophie better from there."

"Not a problem."

Just then the girl's voice trailed down the stairway as she giggled on the phone.

Golden evening light filled the room, so Connie didn't turn on any lamps. She sat on the sofa, and to her surprise, Ethan did, too. There was still plenty of room between them, but it felt more intimate than before. And she liked it.

That liking frightened her, raising images from the grave of her past. Leo hitting her, then apologizing and wanting to make love. Always, always, like some sick twisted game. How many times had she fallen for that?

Too many.

She began curling in on herself, as if in anticipation of an attack. She could feel it in every muscle and struggled to let go of it.

"Am I too close?" Ethan suddenly asked.

She nearly jumped as she looked at him. "What do you mean?"

"I seem to be making you uncomfortable."

"It's not you."

He nodded. Then, after the briefest pause, he said, "Why don't you tell me about it?"

"Why? I show you my scars and you show me yours?" The words sounded so bitter that shock shook Connie. "I'm sorry…"

"It's okay," he said, and everything in his tone said it was. "It's okay. I'm still reacting to threats that aren't there. I know what it's like."

"Yeah. I guess you do."

"It's like your brain gets rewired."

She nodded, still watching him in the golden glow.

"It's hard to turn it back around. When I came back on leave from Iraq, I couldn't drive. I absolutely panicked for a while, thinking every oncoming or parked car might be a bomb."

"That must have been awful."

"It was crazy. I knew it wasn't true, but I couldn't restrain the learned response." He shook his head a little, as if trying to drive away an exasperating bug. "I guess everything in life changes you somehow."

"So it seems."

"I still can't drive." He said it flatly, but even that tone spoke volumes to her. "Well, I can if I have to, but it's an awful lot of effort. More than it's worth most of the time. That's why you caught me hitchhiking."

"I can understand that." And she could. Maybe not in his precise terms, but in her own… Yeah, she could understand.

But the curling inward wouldn't stop, and finally words burst out of her. "Sophie is the best thing in my life," she said, tears starting to run down her cheeks. "My God, if something happened to her…"

He moved closer, drawing her into a gentle embrace, rocking her as if he knew how soothing that motion could be. "Nothing's going to happen," he murmured. "We'll take care of her."

The tears flowed silently, as if she couldn't release the pain and terror enough to sob. Water seeping over a dam that held back the huge lake of terrible things that had never ceased to haunt her.

She felt guilty. The man holding her had been through far worse. Endured far worse. That thing about not being able to drive a car was only the tip of his iceberg, and she knew it. Yet he had the strength to try to protect her daughter. To hold her and offer comfort.

In the midst of it all, she realized what a crabbed soul she had become.

"My God," she said, pulling away and hunting for the box of tissues she always kept on the end table. Finding it by feel, she pulled out a wad and scrubbed her face.

"What?" he asked.

"Sophie… She's never known her father. It's like with you. I took her away from him and made sure he couldn't even see her on supervised visitation. What if she's not as understanding as you? What if she grows up to hate me for that?"

Several heartbeats passed before he answered. He seemed to be choosing his words with care. "Do you think," he asked slowly, "that it would have been good for her to visit her father in prison? Good for her to ask questions about it at such a young age?"

"God! How did you know about Leo going to prison?"

"Micah." He touched her shoulder briefly. Then he moved back to his end of the couch, giving her space.

She needed that space, and she hated needing it. She wanted the comfort he offered, yet it terrified her. Finally she asked the most dreaded question. "Did you ever hate your mother for what she did? Ever? Did you ever resent your father for not knowing?"

"I'm human," he said. "I felt some ugly things, sure. Mostly when I was younger. As I grew older, I understood better. My mother used to have a saying. It helps."

"And that was?"

"The secret to happiness is wanting what you have, not what you wish you had."

Connie nodded, wiping her face again. "That's good advice."

"Not always easy to follow, but it's a good guide-post." He fell silent and thoughtful as the golden light began to fade from the living room. When he spoke again, it was to express volumes in a few words. "Sometimes it's impossible to want what you have."

She drew a sharp breath, sensing the anguish those calm words covered. The urge to try to soothe him in some way nearly overwhelmed her, but she didn't have a clue what to do or say.

"I guess," he said after a moment, "the thing you need to keep in mind is that even the worst things pass eventually. Everything passes."

She suspected he might know more about that than most, given what he'd done and where he'd been. Impulsively, she reached out and took his hand. He didn't pull away but let her squeeze his fingers gently.

At that exact instant, Sophie bounded into the room, waving her cell phone and nearly hopping up and down. Connie swiftly released Ethan's hand.

"Mom, Mom, Jody wants me to come over to spend the night tonight! Can I, please?"

Everything inside Connie shrieked *no!* but she held her tongue, trying to deal with the terror that swamped her and respond rationally. "I don't know…"

"Aww, Mom, I'll be safe there, and we'll have so much fun."

Connie fought the battle that every parent faces sooner or later, though in this case the threat was real, not imagined. In the end, after nearly biting a hole in her lip, she said, "Okay. But I'm driving you over there and picking you up in the morning, and under no circumstances are you to go anywhere without Jody's mom."

Sophie let out a shriek of delight and began babbling to Jody on the phone that she'd be over as soon as she got her pajamas and sleeping bag. A second later she was running up the stairs.

"That was brave," Ethan remarked.

"Or foolish." Connie shook her head. "I'm overreacting. She'll be okay with Jody's family."

"Of course she will. One thing you can say about creeps like this is that as a general rule they prefer their victims to be alone and unprotected. She'll be neither."

Gratitude warmed Connie. "Thanks."

"Don't thank me. You're doing the hard job."

"I just hope I'm doing it right. I guess you get the night off. Want me to take you up to see Micah?"

He shook his head. "We talked some this afternoon. Some things just take time, Connie. We're taking our time."

"All right, then. Help yourself to anything you want." She rose. "It'll only take me ten minutes to run Sophie over there."

He nodded. "I'll be fine. You just go."

She thought about inviting him to ride along, then realized that would mean getting into a car, and she suspected that being a passenger probably was only marginally more comfortable for him than driving, despite all his hitchhiking. As a passenger, if he had a flashback at least he couldn't be in control of the vehicle.

Sophie came bouncing down the stairs with her sleeping bag and backpack. "I'm ready!"

Ethan smiled. "I guess so."

Connie looked at Sophie and started smiling, too. This child was so precious, so full of life. Her heart swelled with love. "Let's go, sweetie."

Behind her, Ethan sat staring into the darkening living room.

Chapter 10

While Connie was gone, Ethan stepped outside to walk around the house again. His training had built a restlessness into him, and he still struggled to realize that war no longer surrounded him. The thing with Sophie was keeping him on his toes, which he supposed was delaying his readjustment a bit.

Not that he blamed anyone for that. He actually felt good about having something useful to do, something he'd been lacking since he'd been shipped home on a stretcher from Afghanistan. He didn't remember much about being wounded, and the pain that plagued him had become a background noise to his days.

He still didn't fully understand why he was receiving a discharge. People with worse injuries returned to combat or took support positions of some kind. But somehow, because of the decision of some review board, he was out.

He struggled with that. He worried about his unit all the time. A sense of failure pervaded his every waking moment, just as nightmares haunted his dreams. He didn't *feel* as if he had a problem of that magnitude, but apparently others thought differently.

You have inoperable shrapnel embedded near your spine. It hadn't affected him yet, other than to cause pain, but one of the doctors had said that it would be years, if ever, before the body's protective mechanisms immobilized it or even ejected it. Until then, the wrong move could paralyze him.

And maybe that was all it was. Maybe they felt he could endanger his unit. One wrong move and he could become an instant paraplegic. Yeah, that could be a problem, all right, but no more of a problem than if it happened because of a wound on the spot.

He paused, looking up at the stars, noting that here in town he couldn't see very many. Not nearly as many as he had seen at night in Afghanistan. Most people in this country probably had almost no idea anymore of how many stars were up there, how many could be seen in the inky blackness of true night. He knew he'd been amazed when he'd looked up from the mountains of Afghanistan the first few times.

Sighing, he continued his perimeter check. He wondered if the good memories would ever begin to replace the bad. These days, his brain functioned like a bad TV show, with almost subliminal flashes of people being torn apart, buddies dying, and all the rest of it. It was as if no matter what he was doing or thinking about, some nasty director would flash up an image so fast he almost didn't catch it.

Except he knew what they were. He didn't have to wonder what had just zipped past his mind's eye. Some things were burned too deeply into memory to escape awareness that easily.

Time, they said. It would just take time, and maybe some therapy. He'd tried the therapy while he recuperated but found it pointless. The guy he had talked to didn't have any direct experience. Oh, he tried, even offering medication, but how could you discuss something worse than the worst horror movie with someone who hadn't even seen *The Exorcist?*

Smiling grimly, he finished his circumnavigation of the house, aware that if this were his post, he would be ripping out a lot of concealing shrubbery and cutting down a few trees that came way too close to the roof.

But this wasn't a military post, and he wasn't preparing for a Taliban incursion. Drawing that distinction seemed to be getting a little easier, and for that he gave thanks.

Inside again, he glanced at his watch. Connie had been gone more than ten minutes. A man who had learned that tardiness could be a sign of catastrophe found it hard to remember that she had probably just stopped to talk with Jody's mother for a few minutes.

God, this living in two worlds was going to drive him nuts.

The phone rang, and he hesitated only a moment before answering it.

"Hi, Ethan, this is Julia. Is my daughter there?"

He felt a smile tug at the corners of his mouth as he heard laughter in the background. "Sorry, ma'am, she took Sophie over to spend the night at Jody's. She should be back any minute. Do you want her to call?"

"Oh, that's not necessary. Just tell her I won't be home tonight. The girls have decided to have an old-fashioned pajama party."

"Hey, that's great," he said with as much warmth as he could muster. "Have fun."

"I will. Sally will bring me home in the morning." Then Julia paused, her voice taking on a different note. "Take care of my girls for me, Ethan. Please."

"I intend to."

When he hung up, he felt oddly revitalized. As if he had his orders now and knew what to do.

He heard Connie pull into the driveway and come through the kitchen door. He heard the lock click behind her; then she returned to the darkened living room.

"Ethan?"

"I just realized something," he said without preamble.

"What's that?"

"That someone else has been organizing my life for so long, I don't know how to get on without orders."

She came farther into the room but didn't switch on a light. "That must stink."

"In a way it does. In another way it's good."

"How so?"

He turned toward her. "It's another challenge. I need challenge."

"I see." Leaning over, she switched on a light at the end of the sofa. It wasn't terribly bright, but it blocked all view of the world beyond the windows and revealed them to one another.

"Your mother called. She said she and her friends are going to have a pajama party. She'll be back in the morning."

At that Connie laughed. "Those women. They're in their second childhood. It's so neat."

"Yeah."

Her eyes came back to him, searching his face. "Didn't you have decisions to make in the service?"

"Plenty. But they were always directed at completing my assignment. My orders."

She nodded. "I hadn't thought of that. And you've been feeling at loose ends without an assignment."

"Basically, yes."

He made a conscious effort to relax and sat on the couch again. "That's probably part of the reason I feel so out of it. I've lived one lifestyle since I was eighteen, and now it's gone."

"That's gotta be tough, Ethan."

"No. I just needed to understand what was happening. Part of it, at least."

"Is that why you were so ready to step in and help with Sophie?"

"Partly. But most of it is that nothing makes me madder than a guy who wants to hurt children." His hands clenched on his lap, and he let them. "But don't think this is some kind of therapy for me."

"I didn't think it was. If anything, I thought it might make your reentry more difficult."

That surprised him. He looked at her and felt an unexpected surge of something so primal and elemental that it shocked him. Urges he hadn't had time or room for since the war began, not even when he came home on leave, because even then he was too busy just coping with what now seemed like an alternative universe.

Despite his preference for silence, for dealing with things in the privacy of his own mind, he started talking.

"Coming home doesn't feel like coming home anymore."

She nodded encouragingly.

"I don't know if you can understand, but I walk around feeling naked because I don't have an M-16 in my arms. It's as if I'm exposed to every danger in the world, and I don't even have a knife to pull."

"Oh, Ethan…"

He made a slight gesture, asking her to just let him continue.

"I know it's wrong. I know it's a kind of mental instability, but there it is. I come home, and I feel adrift. Purposeless. Naked. Being at home…it's like visiting another planet. I felt less out of place the first time I was shipped overseas."

"They say that Peace Corps volunteers adjust to their new countries more easily than they adjust to their return here. There must be a reason for it."

He sighed. "Sorry, I'm dumping."

"Dump away."

He rose and began pacing the living room slowly. He paused just once to draw the heavy curtains closed over the sheers. "It's like I know things other people can't understand. Some folks I know think that makes them better. Hell, I know a SEAL who's so full of his own superiority because he's been through life-and-death situations, because he knows things…he scorns civilians."

"Do *you?*"

"No. That's the thing. I took on this job because I had the stupid idea that I'd be protecting other people from having to know, not because it would make me special. But now I can't come home."

He hated showing his weakness the instant the words escaped him. He wanted to snatch them back and rip them to shreds with his bare hands, because he had no business whining about this shit. No business at all.

But before self-disgust could conquer him, he had a warm, soft woman in his arms, holding him tightly as if she wanted to anchor him in the storm.

"Oh, Ethan… Ethan…"

Her voice seemed to call to him from across an

abyss, the abyss that separated him from his current reality. The yawning abyss of places he had been, horrors he had seen, evils he had done.

I'm not worthy.

The words had been rattling around in his head for a long time, but now they rang loud with a truth he couldn't ignore. He'd bloodied his hands, whether for good or ill he no longer knew. How could he know? Clausewitz had written that war was politics by other means. He couldn't judge the politics. And after he got to Afghanistan, he couldn't even tell any longer if the cost of chasing the Taliban and Al Qaeda was worth it. Because he saw the cost day in and day out. The cost in innocent lives, which hadn't stopped on 9/11.

His job over there had been to win hearts and minds while pushing back the forces of darkness. He wished he could be sure that was all he had done.

But in a war without uniforms, how could you always tell?

You couldn't. So you had to live with the stain and wonder forever.

His hands weren't clean, might never be clean, but he wrapped them around Connie and held her as tight as he would a lifeline. He needed the affirmation as much as he'd ever needed anything.

Odd, he'd wanted it from Micah, but he found, instead, that it mattered more coming from this woman, an innocent who had never sullied herself. It didn't make logical sense, but emotionally he felt as if she was offering forgiveness.

He just didn't know if he could accept it. Didn't know if he deserved it.

Soon, even that question began to slip away, replaced by deepening awareness of the body pressed against his. Sexual desire, long held at bay by the need for survival that could be lost in a moment's inattention, began to pace within him like too-long-caged wolf.

Nor was it simply desire for any woman. No. He desired *this* woman and no other. *Her* warmth, *her* curves, awakened him. It would have been so easy just to give in and carry her to the floor, but conscience rose, reminding him of her vulnerability.

Just as he would have released her, she lifted her head and her lips found his. The brush of a butterfly wing, so light he barely felt it, but it sent an electric jolt to the farthest cells of his body.

He almost swore. Like Frankenstein's monster, lightning was bringing him to life. She deserved so much better.

But the thought never fully formed, because she moved against him, just a little, a soft murmur escaping her as she sought deeper contact with his mouth.

He couldn't resist. He needed this kiss more than he had needed anything in his life. He lowered his head, pressing his mouth to hers, gently at first, then more deeply, as she welcomed him.

His groin throbbed with forgotten longing as his body woke to new possibilities that seemed to offer salvation of some kind.

He ached deeply, needing…needing…

"Ethan…"

His name sounded like a prayer as she whispered it. Buried parts of his very being burst free of their bonds, reminding him that he was a living, breathing man like any other.

It would have been less painful to rip off his own skin, but he pulled away, conscience piercing him like a dagger.

She looked at him from sleepy, worried eyes. "Ethan?"

"I don't want to hurt you, and I'm afraid I might. I can't even trust *myself*, Connie. How can I ask anyone else to trust me?"

A wounded look pinched her eyes, and finally she nodded. "You're right," she said thickly. "I can't trust myself, either. I've been avoiding men since Leo because I know I'm not a decent judge, and…" She turned and fled.

He listened to her feet pound as she ran upstairs to her bedroom, and he hated himself

Not hurt her? He just had.

Chapter 11

Although it was still early evening, Connie got ready for bed. She went through the motions automatically, trying to fight down feelings of hurt and despair that really had nothing to do with Ethan. All he had done was remind her of Leo. That wasn't his fault.

In fact, she told herself as she brushed her teeth, he had been kind enough to protect her from herself.

So why did she feel so bad?

A quick shower washed off the day's grit but not the day's worries. Nothing could wash those away, and she seemed to nurture them sometimes. Oh, not her concern about Sophie. That was as real as a worry could be. But other stuff. Her past. Her constant tension, as if she feared being beaten again. As she knew only too well, not even packing a gun could protect her from that, not when she loved someone. Or thought she did.

Some old country song floated into her mind as she climbed into a cotton nightshirt. Something about it not really being love if it tore you apart.

Great line. But as someone who had been there, she knew the other side of that one. Leo had never loved her in the true sense of the word, but she had sure as hell loved him. At least until fear pushed out the love.

She flopped onto the bed and reached for the TV remote on her night table, then hunted for something that would occupy her mind enough to keep her from thinking. She'd been thinking for too many years as it was, but tonight she doubted she would be able to even manage to read a book. Everything about her felt scattered to the four winds.

No crime shows, too close to her job. No romances, too painful. Ghosts? Didn't she already have enough of her own? Comedy didn't seem very funny tonight. News? No, there might be something there to remind her of the very things she was trying to forget.

Finally she settled on a lightweight British police procedural. Amusing, devoid of ugliness, very different from the real thing.

She switched off the light and settled in, hoping the eccentric British characters would suffice to distract her.

Unfortunately, her body wasn't quite ready to quiet

down. She wondered if Leo had ever aroused her the way Ethan just had. If he ever had, she couldn't remember now.

Somehow she doubted it. Something about Ethan was magical, tormented soul though he was. A pang seized her heart as she remembered what he'd shared with her. Awful. Absolutely awful. He needed a magic wand, but the universe didn't hand those out to anyone.

Somehow you just had to keep muddling through, trying to mend yourself or put the bad stuff behind you. All a therapist could do, she had learned through experience, was give you the tools to do one or the other. Maybe that was the hardest thing of all: learning you had to be your own healer.

She rolled over on the bed, her body restless with hunger she couldn't erase, hunger so strong it almost hurt. Her loins ached with it. Her breasts had become exquisitely sensitive to every movement of her night-gown across her nipples.

She didn't want this. She had a child to think of, and her mother, in addition to herself, and the agenda didn't include playing with fire.

But she burned, anyway, television forgotten.

Could just one night be that dangerous? Why couldn't she scratch the itch and move on? Other people did.

Why, she wondered almost angrily, couldn't she enjoy the most basic human contact? Did she feel she had to punish herself for one major mistake? What made her so different from anyone else? Who said she could never trust herself again?

She did.

She had devised all the rules for her current life, maybe in reaction to her complete lack of control in her relationship with Leo. Maybe now she felt she had to control *everything*.

Talk about an impossibility! Apparently she couldn't even protect her own daughter.

The phone beside her bed rang, and she reached for it, expecting to hear Sophie's voice bubbling over with giggles about how much fun they were having.

Instead, she heard a chilling voice.

"She's a beautiful child, Connie."

Her veins turned to ice as she slammed the phone down on the cradle. No! *No!*

Then she screamed.

"Ethan!"

Ethan bounded up the stairs three at a time and burst into Connie's room. In the flickering light from her television, she was pulling frantically at the phone cord, trying to yank it out of the wall.

"Connie?"

"It was him," she sobbed. "It was *him!*"

"Who?"

"The man who wants Sophie. He said she's a beautiful child. Oh, God, oh, God, oh, God…"

Ethan crossed the room and took her into his arms, at once confining her gently and supporting her. "Shh… Shh…"

"He called. Oh, God, he called! Sophie…" She

began shoving against Ethan, trying to escape. "I have to call and see if she's all right. Sophie... Oh, my God..."

"Shh," he said more sharply. "I'm here, and I'll help. Is the phone still plugged in?"

"I don't know. Oh, God..."

He lifted the receiver and heard the dial tone. "What's the number?"

She managed to gasp it out, then grabbed the receiver as he dialed for her.

"Hi," said the cheerful voice of Jody's mom, Enid.

"Enid, this is Connie. A man just called. Is Sophie okay?"

"She's okay, Connie. My God, she's okay. She's right here with the other girls, eating popcorn and watching *The Little Mermaid.* Are you sure it was the guy?"

At that, Connie collapsed onto the edge of her bed and began sobbing. "He talked about Sophie. He said she was beautiful."

"Oh, sweetie," Enid said, her voice taut with concern and an echo of Connie's fear. "I won't let her out of my sight. John's here, too, and he's keeping an eye on them. And between you and me, he's loaded for bear. But...would you feel better if you took her home?"

"No!" Somehow the idea of bringing Sophie here right after that man had called was even more terrifying. "No. She's probably safer there. I'll call Gage and let him know what happened. Don't be surprised if you see a deputy out front."

"Good. That was my next suggestion. Now, you're sure you're okay if she stays here?"

Connie forced herself to breathe. "I'm okay with it. He called here. Maybe he doesn't know she's there."

"No reason he should, unless he has a better intelligence network than the CIA. Which probably isn't saying much. We're not letting the girls out of the house, and John has already said he's staying up all night to keep an eye on them. Not that I expect either of us will sleep, anyway. The girls are having too much fun."

"Okay," Connie said shakily. "Okay. I just had to be sure."

"Of course you did," Enid said comfortingly. "My God, I've been scared to death ever since the guy talked to the girls. I just sound like I'm calm. Look, I'll call you again in an hour or so if you want. I can keep you posted all night."

"Oh, Enid, that's too much!"

"No, it isn't," Enid said firmly. "I know how I'd be feeling in your shoes. I'll give you updates. But don't get worried if I'm a little late, because these girls are keeping me busy. Now they want brownies. Good thing I like to bake."

Connie managed a choked little laugh. "You're a good woman, Enid. An angel."

"Nah. I'm just a mom. You hang in there. John and I are on guard."

"Thank you. Thank you so much."

"You'd do the same for me. Now relax and try not to climb the walls."

Connie's hand shook as she replaced the receiver.

Ethan stood not a foot away, waiting. "Everything's okay," she said.

"Good." He squatted to her eye level, an exotic, mysterious-looking man with eyes nearly as dark as midnight, yet strangely comforting. "Tell me everything he said."

"That was all. He said Sophie was a beautiful child."

"Okay, then let's think about why he would call."

She realized he was trying to get her to think like a police officer, instead of a mother. And he was right. She needed all her wits about her. "To scare me. To let me know the threat is still there."

"That would be my guess. So what does that mean? It sure won't make it any easier for him to get to Sophie, will it?"

Her eyes felt full of glue, hot and burning, as she met his gaze. "No," she whispered. "It'll make it harder."

"So maybe we need to think about what *that* means."

She nodded slowly. "I've got to call Gage."

He waited while she did, and Gage promised to dispatch some officers to Enid and John's house to keep an eye out. He also wanted to place one at Connie's, but she told him no. "Just watch the kids, Gage. I'm a deputy, too, remember. I'll take care of myself."

When she hung up, Ethan still stood there. Then he asked, "Want to come downstairs for coffee or something? Or are you better here?"

"I need to move."

"Let's go, then."

He led the way downstairs. She carried a robe with her, but it was too warm to put on. Nor did she care in the least that she was in a nightshirt. Trivialities no longer existed for her.

Surprisingly, the homey scent of coffee brewing helped pull her back from the precipice of a break-down. Rationality began to reassert itself. Gradually her breathing slowed and her heart calmed. Ethan sat beside her, close enough to reach for her if she needed comforting, but far enough not to crowd her. No reason that should surprise her. He'd probably dealt with more terror and horror in a few years than most people did in a lifetime.

"He's after me," she said presently.

"In what way?" The question, however, seemed to suggest that he had an idea.

"He wants me scared. He's trying to get to me."

"I agree. Right now it seems that way. Can you handle it?"

"Him scaring me? Only if Sophie isn't at risk."

Ethan nodded "You're a strong woman. If we could be certain he intends Sophie no harm, that would be the end of it."

"But there's no way to know!"

"That's the devil of it. I won't kid you, Connie. This is the worst-possible kind of threat."

"What do you mean?"

"Well, in Afghanistan, we might meet a group of village chieftains who claimed to be all gung-ho for getting rid of Al Qaeda and the Taliban, then the next day we'd drive into their village to provide medical care or help rebuild a school, and get attacked. When you don't know where the threat is coming from, or exactly what it's going to be, your options are a mess."

"Yeah." She stared down at the oilcloth-covered table, her hands knotting together until they hurt. "I don't know how to handle this."

"That's what I meant. Is Sophie the target? Are you the target? Are you both the target? What do we most need to guard against?"

"I wish I knew."

"What did this guy sound like?"

"Distant, almost. But there was something else in his tone. I can't put my finger on it."

"Anything familiar? Any recognition?"

"Maybe. Maybe so." But every ounce of her being recoiled at the thought that she might know this creep. She didn't want to believe it possible that someone like that could have crawled into the most distant periphery of her life.

"Okay." He rose and went to get them both coffee.

Connie cradled her mug, but made no attempt to drink. She felt cold, so very cold. The kind of cold no amount of heat could dissipate.

As if he sensed it, Ethan reached for the robe she'd thrown over the back of a chair and draped it over her shoulders. It actually helped a little.

"Connie, who might want to get at you both?"

Everything inside her turned glacial: cold, hard and ready to crack. She whispered, "Leo."

He remained silent, waiting.

Slowly she turned her head to look at him. "Ethan, he got out of jail several months back. But I've changed my name. There's no reason he should have found me."

"Did he know about your uncle living here?"

"God…" She tipped her head back, closing her eyes, loosing a long, despairing sigh. "I didn't think so. I mean, Uncle Nate and I were never that close until I moved here. Leo knew I had family in Wyoming, but I'm pretty sure I never mentioned Nate or Conard County. Leo wasn't the kind of guy to be interested in that stuff, and my maiden name was different. It never occurred to me that he could make a link." She shook her head almost violently. "Damn, I'm stupid. I guess I need to pack up and leave again."

"Not so hasty, there. First of all, you're surrounded by people who want to protect you here. Second, you've got to face the bastard and deal with him."

"I dealt with him once before! Do you know how hard it was to go into a courtroom and describe what he did to me? What I *let* him do to me?"

"You know better than that. You weren't responsible for what he did for you. I don't need to be a shrink to understand how domestic violence works, to understand how helpless and vulnerable it leaves a woman. He tried to blame you for it, but you know better than that, Connie. Or you should. It wasn't your fault."

"That's what everyone says. But I still have to live with the fact that I didn't leave sooner. That I let it go on so long."

"If it were easy to get out of those situations, they wouldn't exist. You get undermined before you know it. And those bastards are really good at making you feel responsible for what they do."

She looked at him. "How do you know so much?"

"Because I've seen it happen. Because I've talked about it with other guys. The military has a lot of domestic-abuse counselors. One of them was a friend of mine. He explained it all to me."

"Okay, so you know the mechanics. But then there are the feelings."

"Trust me, I know about those, too. Maybe you aren't ready to make peace with the fact that you were skillfully manipulated and brainwashed. I can understand that. I'm having problems of my own. But that doesn't change the fact that *he* was responsible, not you." He leaned toward her, his eyes burning. "And you are *not* responsible for what is happening now."

"I *feel* responsible!"

"So? That doesn't make it true. You didn't ask for this. You did everything you could to avoid it. Now it's here, and we're going to deal with it so you can have the life you deserve."

Something in his expression made her shiver. "You wouldn't…"

"Yeah, I'm a trained killer," he said bitterly. "But generally I don't kill unless I have to. I don't just get up on Saturday morning and decide it would be a good day for a murder."

"I didn't mean that!"

"Maybe not."

"You know damn well I didn't. And frankly, if it's Leo terrorizing me and my daughter, I might kill him before you get a chance!"

They glared at each other across twelve inches of space, nerves and wounds so raw in both of them that it didn't matter if they were reacting rationally.

Right then and there everything hurt too much to make sense of it.

Then, without warning, something inside Connie shifted. All of a sudden she felt the hysterical urge to giggle. The laugh started bubbling out of her, totally random, totally without reason, and then, only God knew why, she said, "Make love not war."

His jaw dropped a half inch and his eyes widened; then, just as helplessly, he started laughing, too.

"Where did that come from?" he asked, breathless.

"I don't know!" She couldn't stop laughing. "Where did any of this come from?"

Laughter existed only a millimeter from tears, just as hate was the flip side of love. The strongest emotions occupied the same realms, basic and primal, entangled beyond extrication.

Tears began to stream down Connie's cheeks, and she felt the crash coming. A pit yawned before her, and she didn't know how to step back from it.

But Ethan knew his way around these emotional pitfalls, maybe because he'd survived so many, presenting a stony facade to the world when everything inside him began to crack.

He reached for her, pulling her onto his lap, wrapping her in his strength, pressing her face to his shoulder. She fit as if the space had been created for her.

Staring over her head at the ordinary sights of a kitchen, he saw, instead, distant landscapes, horrible anguish and suffering.

Life could be such a bitch.

But he knew one thing for certain: if he never did another thing with his life, he was going to make this woman and her child safe from this creep.

It was as solemn a vow as any he'd ever taken, filling his heart, touching his soul, giving back purpose and meaning where they had been stripped away.

No matter what it took.

Chapter 12

Connie's laughter had given way to tears, but copious though they were, they fell silently, as if her body were too exhausted to do more than weep. The shoulder of his shirt grew damp, then sopping, as Ethan continued to hold her.

Calm returned slowly, finding its way back one quiet step at a time. Finally Connie lifted a hand and wiped her cheeks. "Sorry."

"No need." He didn't want to let go of her. He wanted to keep her right where she was, as if it were the only way he could protect her. And maybe himself.

Nor did she seem eager to escape his embrace. She rested against him, within the circle of his arms, as if she had found a measure of peace at last.

That wouldn't remain. It never did. But for now, neither of them risked disturbing it.

Reality had its own rules, however, and at last, with a sigh, Connie slid from his lap and back into her own chair. She reached for her coffee, found it cold and went to get a fresh cup.

"Thank you," she said quietly.

"If you can't hunker down with your friends in a firefight, when can you?"

"That's an interesting analogy." She returned to her seat and sipped the coffee.

"This situation qualifies."

"I guess it does." She shook her head, as if trying to wipe away a thought, then looked at him with a pallid smile. "I usually cope better."

"With something like this? I suppose you have a whole lot of experience with this kind of thing?"

At that, her smile broadened a shade. "No, I guess I don't. If Sophie weren't involved… But why even think about it? She *is* involved. That's what's killing me."

"Of course it is. Most of us worry less about ourselves than we do about those we care for."

"You're right." A shiver passed through her—a release of tension, he guessed. "Time to stop being hysterical and start thinking."

He nodded when she looked at him, waiting to hear what she had to say.

"I'm going to start by calling Enid and telling her she doesn't have to call me on and off all night as long as everything is okay. Because I'm damned if I'm going to answer the phone again."

"I could answer for you."

"No. I don't want to give the creep the satisfaction." Rising, she went to the wall phone and dialed Enid's number. In the background, mayhem still reigned.

"Okay," Enid said. "If you're sure. These girls are so wound up, I can guarantee you they won't crash before dawn. And the cops keep prowling around. I think *they're* making me more nervous."

"I appreciate everything, Enid. I really do. But I need to start focusing on why this guy called me and what I should do about it, and honestly, I'd rather not be answering the phone tonight."

"I can see why, honey. Don't give the crud the satisfaction. And if you get concerned, just call. Like I said, we're going to be up all night."

When Connie hung up, she returned to her seat and her coffee. "It's got to be Leo," she announced.

"That's my guess."

"No one else would want to scare both Sophie and me."

"You think he just wants to scare you?"

"Him? I don't know. In the end, guys like him often turn out to be bullies who can't stand up against any show of strength."

Ethan nodded. "Did he say anything threatening at all?"

"No. Just that Sophie was a beautiful child."

"Could he have any other motive?"

"Why would he? He kicked me in the stomach when I was pregnant. Does that sound like a man who wants his child?"

"That sounds like a man who feels threatened."

"Exactly. And maybe now he's angry because I sent him to prison. But I'm not the woman he used to kick around."

"I'm sure you're not."

She looked at Ethan, determination in every line of her. "If it's Leo, we could put his photo out there. At least among the deputies."

"How sure are you?"

She paused thoughtfully. Finally she said, "I'm not a hundred percent sure, but close to it. He only said one thing, which didn't give me much to go on, considering how shocked I was. It was like I lost all sense for a few minutes there."

"Hardly surprising."

"Yeah." Then she astonished him by taking his hand and holding it. "You're a godsend, Ethan."

"No. Just a guy who happened to be in the right place when needed."

Her smile was pinched. "I think you have a worse self-image than I do. And it's not right. I can tell what a good man you are. Yeah, you did some awful things, but you didn't do them alone. You did them because I and every other person in this country asked them of you."

"I don't—"

"Shh," she said gently. "It's true. You were in the

service. You got your orders from this country, and you went. If there's any guilt in what you did, we all share it. All of us. We can't claim lily-white hands because we didn't put on a uniform. Not in this country."

He didn't respond, seeming to lack the words.

"You know it's true, Ethan. You do the dirty work we ask you to do. Whatever gloss we put on it, however high we hold the flag and however loud we cry the justifications, you and your fellow soldiers are just carrying out our will. Sometimes you'll be sure it was absolutely right. But I suspect that in all wars the people on the front lines often wind up wondering what they've done and what it makes them."

"Connie—"

"Listen to me. Just remember, when you walk down a street, that you didn't do a damn thing all the rest of us walking those same streets didn't ask of you. Didn't send you there to do."

Her grip on his hand had grown vise tight, and he squeezed back. Finally he gave a short, mirthless laugh and said, "I guess this is a night for therapy."

"Or a night for putting things into perspective. You tried to help me see I wasn't responsible for what Leo did. Well, you need to understand that just because you were the tip of the spear doesn't make you any more responsible than the rest of us, the spear throwers."

For a few moments he seemed about to argue with her, but then tension seeped from him. Before she knew what to expect, she was swept up into his arms and being carried up the stairs as if she weighed nothing at all.

She didn't make a sound, didn't offer a protest. How could she? Nothing had ever felt so right as being in his arms.

He carried her into her darkened bedroom, where the TV still flickered, and laid her on her bed. Then he stretched out beside her, fully clothed, and pulled her close, as if he wanted their bodies to melt together. She managed to wrap one arm around him, feeling the breadth and strength of his back. Feeling the wonder of him in every cell of her being.

"This'll sound crazy," he said huskily.

"Tell me."

"You just said something to me that made more sense than anything anyone's said in a long time— except for something Micah said the other day."

"What did he say?"

"He told me the past was past, that if I wanted atonement, I had to find it in today. And that if I had nightmares, I had to build new dreams."

She drew a sharp breath. "That's so true! So beautiful. Oh, Ethan, I need to remember that, too."

"I know. We're not so very different, in some ways."

"No, we're not." She tightened her hold on him. "When was the last time someone told you how beautiful you are?"

"Me?" He gave an embarrassed laugh.

"You," she repeated. "Not just the way you look, although you probably have no idea what a handsome man you are, but in other ways. The first night you spent here, I felt something about you, something in the air around you. You were saying something about having studied shamanism and being a bit of a mystic. I don't remember exactly. I just know I could feel it all around you, as if you're a special spirit."

"Not me. I'm an ordinary man."

"No, you're more than that." She sighed and shifted so that her head was cradled comfortably on his shoulder. "I used to think we were beings of light unwillingly tethered to the ground."

"And now?"

"I still think we're beings of light, but we aren't tethered unwillingly."

"No?"

She tilted her head so she could see his face. "No," she repeated. "We came here for this. For something beautiful we can experience no other way. Holding and being held. Comforting and being comforted. Skin touching skin across the abyss of seeming separateness."

He closed his eyes as if absorbing her words. "You should try poetry."

"Not me. It's just what I feel sometimes. Transcendence through our very limitations. Tell me you haven't felt it."

He nodded slowly. "Rarely," he said presently. "Too rarely. But yes, I've felt it."

"These are the moments we exist for, Ethan."

He cradled her even closer, if that was possible, and

rocked her gently. The motion was soothing, seeming to lift her to another level.

This wasn't possible, she warned herself, but the warning seemed distant and faint. She knew she would never trust fully again, and she knew that Ethan would undoubtedly move on until he found a life that suited him. They were too wounded to build anything between them.

So if she gave in to the longings building in her, it would be for a night. A single night. There would be no future in it.

Oddly, that seemed to free her. It banished all the fears from her marriage that had been holding her back. There was nothing to fear here, because this wouldn't be a commitment. Nothing to upset her carefully established balance.

In Ethan's arms, she felt herself grow weightless, as if she were rising to the heavens, above it all, safe from it all. Magic surrounded her, sheltered her, filled her.

She hardly felt herself move as she turned her face up, seeking his kiss.

When it came, gentleness came with it, a tender touching of lips that spoke not of hunger but a different kind of need, a more important one.

She responded in kind, shedding her shell, reveling in the freedom to just experience and share. Savoring the deep sense of safety that must have been coming from him, because it surely didn't come from her.

He began to stoke her back, firmly but gently,

shoulder to small of back, over and over until she understood why cats purr. A soft moan escaped her, saying all that words couldn't.

Slowly his hand slipped lower, pressing her rounded bottom and bringing her into the cradle of his hips. Now she could feel his need, too, as well as her own, and the feeling was so good, so good…

She had never known a man could be so hard all over, nor that his hardness against her softness could be so enticing. Every inch of Ethan had been honed for action, and awareness of that carried her to some elemental place inside her where nothing existed except man and woman, woman and man. Identity slipped away, succumbing to urges as old as time.

They fit together as if they had been created for this. His kiss grew deeper, and her hips rocked in response, trying to get closer to him, trying to find the answer to her growing ache.

His mouth left hers, tracing a path lower, along the slender column of her neck, awakening new nerve endings, sending a shiver through her. Warm, soft lips, hard body, heat…passing chill, all of it descending through her to her very center, where it fed the growing, hardening ache inside.

The cotton of her nightgown provided no barrier as he moved lower, tracing her collarbone with his tongue, slipping straps away to bare her shoulders to his chase.

He rolled her gently onto her back, as if sensing she was utterly open to him. First his lips, then his tongue, found the stiffened buds of her nipples through the thin cotton, causing her to give a soft cry of delight and need.

He teased her, light brushes and kisses while the cotton grew damp, until she writhed in helpless thrall to the hunger he drew from her. Only then did he close his mouth over her, drawing her in, sucking gently in a rhythm that caused an echoing tightening between her legs.

His hand slipped up the outside of her leg, drawing her nightgown with it, exposing her to the cool air and, wonderfully, to his touch. The first brush of his fingers at the apex of her thighs was a mere hint, barely stirring the nest, yet causing her to shudder breathlessly.

Yes, that was what she wanted. More of that. Harder. She lifted her hips to find what she needed, but he pulled his hand away, denying her. Tormenting her in the most beautiful way imaginable.

"Ethan…" A sharp whisper, and she reached for his powerful shoulders, trying to draw him closer, but he resisted. His mouth moved to her other breast, drawing her desire out like a taut string ready to be plucked to create the most perfect note.

The realms she visited then were places she had never imagined could exist. Her entire body became his instrument, played for both her pleasure and his.

Then, almost without her realizing it, her nightgown vanished over her head. Naked, exposed, vulnerable…

And enthralled with the beauty of it all.

"Ethan," she said on a sigh, letting him have

whatever he chose to take, because every taking was a giving beyond any but the rawest comprehension.

He lifted her to the mountain peaks, and she soared willingly with him.

A dark moment came, a moment when he vanished. She struggled against the web of heat and wonder that held her to try to find him, but then he returned, and when he did, she felt his smooth, hot skin along her side.

"Oh, Ethan…" She turned toward him then, wrapping her arms around his shoulders, surrendering herself to him.

She belonged completely to him.

Chapter 13

It had been too long. Ethan had buried this part of himself for the last four years, using his stateside rotations to try to sort himself out, not wanting to turn to easy women, absolutely refusing to draw a better woman into the mess of his life.

Now here he was with a good, decent woman, feeling a hunger for her that took him by surprise in its strength. There was no way he could have pulled back now. All that he had tried to spare himself and others turned to dust.

He needed this beyond all reason and caution, although at some point he had realized that Connie wanted this just as much. Just these beautiful, glorious moments of man meeting woman in the most basic way, the way the human race had always dissolved its alone-ness.

He had been alone for a long time now. Intense as friendships could be in battle, this was a kind of union that could be replaced by no other. It reached out to fill places nothing else could.

He felt her shiver and tremble against him, felt her vulnerability as a blessing, felt her hunger and need meet and match his own, validating him at his deepest levels, way below thought.

The magic that bound her surrounded him, as well. He felt as if rainbows danced along his arms and zinged through his nerves. The voice of thunder roared through him.

Each shiver or sigh he drew from her was a gift that tightened his throat. When her nails dug into his shoulders, trying to pull him closer, he knew joy and triumph that he could give such a gift.

And when at last he levered himself over her and slowly sank into her welcoming heat, he knew a kind of salvation.

Then everything vanished as they rode the wave higher and higher, until they exploded together in a place beyond the stars.

They lay together in a hot, damp heap, limbs sprawled across each other, breaths slowing, heartbeats steadying. The TV still flickered, but the sound was too low to penetrate their cocoon of satisfaction and wonder.

She trailed her fingers lightly along his arm, as if re-assuring herself of his reality. He held her hips close, as if he couldn't bear for her to move away.

A long, shuddering sigh escaped her, and she pressed a kiss to his chest, near one small nipple. A shiver passed through him in response.

The hunger, fulfilled, had not vanished but merely simmered.

"Are you okay?" he asked. His voice rumbled deep in his chest.

She kissed him again. "I never knew it was possible to feel this wonderful."

"Me, neither." Sad to say, yet true. Something special had just happened here, but he wasn't ready to think about that.

Maybe he was even *reluctant* to think about it. Better to accept some things rather than analyze them.

Cooling now, he reached with one arm for the sheet and pulled it up. She settled more comfortably against him, displaying no desire to end these moments. That relieved him. He could have understood it if she had wanted to run. They had crossed lines he suspected neither of them had ever intended to.

Yet here they were, and he wanted it to end no more than she did. Comfort, he thought, could be such a rare thing, yet he'd found it here in this woman's arms. He hoped she had found it in his.

Midnight was creeping close on stealthy feet when Connie asked, "Are you hungry? I am."

"I guess I am, but only a little."

"Do you want real food, or will dessert do you?"

He smiled into her fragrant hair. "Dessert sounds fabulous."

She pushed him playfully. "Food first, then me."

He laughed and followed her out of the bed, pulling on his T-shirt and shorts while she knotted her robe around herself.

As he followed her down the stairs, he noted how small and fragile she appeared, in direct contrast to the iron strength of her spirit and will. A powerful urge to wipe the sorrows from her life rose in him.

When she bent to look in the refrigerator, he noted the perfect curves of her bottom, and his hands remembered the way her flesh had felt.

"We have strawberry pie," she said.

"What's that?"

"My mother's concoction." She pulled out a pie plate with a plastic lid. "Trust me, it's good. Strawberry gelatin full of real strawberries on a graham-cracker crust. Topped with whipped cream and more strawberries."

"That does sound good." It sounded like heaven, in fact. "I'm sure I've never had anything like it."

She flashed a grin and cut him a generous portion of the pie. "It's not as high in sugar or fat as you'd expect, not with all the strawberries. And she's gentle with the whipped cream."

Given the life he'd been living, such concerns were pretty much foreign to him. Flavor was everything, and he'd had little enough of that for a while. A surprising number of soldiers in the field had to be reminded to eat, despite their heightened need for calories. Even so, most lost twenty or thirty pounds on a tour.

When he sank his teeth into his first bite of pie, he closed his eyes in sheer bliss, shutting out anything that might distract him from the taste. Fresh strawberries, perfectly balancing the sweetness all around them. When he finally allowed himself to swallow, he said, "Tell Julia I want to marry her."

"You can tell her yourself. But," she added coquettishly, "I know how to make this, too."

"Then I'll marry both of you. You have no idea how long it's been since I tasted something like this."

"I can guess. And there's plenty more."

He smiled and raised another forkful to his mouth. "Over there," he said before he put it in his mouth, "we don't get anything even a tenth as tasty as this. MREs, of course. Food we cook at our firebase, but none of us is a great chef, including the chef."

She giggled a little at that.

"Well, he doesn't have a lot to work with. We have to bring in all the food, so everything's pretty much dried or canned. Eating is more a duty than a pleasure most of the time."

"I'm sorry."

He shrugged. "Most of the world is in the same straits. In fact, we're better off than most, even if it's all in cans and boxes. More variety."

She nodded. "I can't imagine the hardship those people suffer."

"Most people can't. It's beyond imagining. You have to see it, live it. Yet the wonderful thing, the truly wonderful thing, is how few of them feel they're living in hardship, except in terms of the war." He paused, then shook his head.

"They must consider you a striking figure," she remarked.

At that his mouth twisted wryly. "I've been mistaken for bin Laden a few times. Despite my uniform."

"Oh, that must be something."

"Oh, yeah. Never for more than a few seconds. We favor different headwear, of course, and we really don't look alike. In all honesty, I don't know why it happened."

"I don't see a resemblance. Maybe some people have never seen his photo, just heard how tall he is."

"That's the only thing that would explain it."

He savored another mouthful of pie. "Damn, this is good."

She pulled the pie pan closer and sliced another piece, sliding it onto his plate.

"Whoa," he said.

She shook her head. "My guess is you're beneath your fighting weight, and anyway, Julia will be thrilled you like it. The best compliment to the cook is eating."

She turned her head, a mistake, because all of a sudden she became uneasily aware of the lurking night, held at bay only by the thin glass of the windows. Ordinarily she loved the night, but not now. Not when a threat was hovering over her daughter.

"Excuse me," she said. "I need to check on Sophie."

He nodded, his gaze following her as she went to the phone and dialed.

"Hi, Enid, it's Connie."

"Hi, kiddo. Well, we're into *Cinderella,* the girls ate all the brownies, if you can believe it, and now there are rumblings about popcorn. It's all good, Connie. Honestly."

"Thanks, Enid. Is it okay if I check again later?"

"Any time, Connie. Like I said, this is going to be an all-nighter. The later it gets, the more awake they seem."

Connie replaced the receiver and found Ethan watching her. "Everything's all right."

He nodded, saying nothing, returning his attention to his plate as if wishing to give her a moment of privacy, one she seemed to need.

Looking at her hands, she realized she was shaking. Not good. She stuffed them in the pockets of her robe and returned to the table, trying to act as if everything hadn't all just come crashing back.

"I'm sorry," she said.

"Nothing to be sorry for."

She bit her lip. "I just realized something."

"What's that?"

"Leo made me feel as if I needed to apologize for everything. I'm still doing it."

He nodded, pushing his plate to one side. Hardly a crumb remained. "That's a damn shame, because I can't see anything you need to apologize for. Not one thing."

"I've been working on that," she admitted. "My mother hates it when I keep on apologizing."

"I don't hate it," he replied, "but I think it's sad you feel that way."

"Maybe it's more habit than anything."

"Maybe."

She watched as he rose and took care of the dishes, washing them and putting them in the rack. Then he put the pie away and wiped the table down. She supposed it was his military training, but she liked it. Leo had never done anything like that in the whole time she'd lived with him.

Together they climbed the stairs and returned to her bedroom, where they lay in the dark, embracing. The sexual fever had passed for now, replaced by an equally urgent need for comfort and closeness.

"I've been alone for too long," he said quietly. She could feel his voice rumble deep in his chest.

"Even with your buddies?"

"That's different. That's an intense community. We depend on each other for our very lives. But it's different."

She gave him a little squeeze and waited for him to continue.

"There's a special bond," he continued slowly, then cleared his throat, as if he were finding it difficult to speak. "You know your buddies always have your back. You know you always have theirs. I don't know if I can really explain it. But it's like many have said, when you're in the foxhole, you're not fighting for principles, country or any such abstract thing, you're fighting for the guy next to you."

"I can understand that," she murmured.

"But there's something more. We were dedicated to something, Connie. Something bigger than us. Something we were willing to die for. And it wasn't just the guy beside us who depended on us. It was—this is going to sound nuts, given all that's happened—we were dedicated to helping those people in every way we could. We didn't want to abandon them to the darkness again. We wanted to save lives, improve lives, make sure little girls could go to school, and that babies didn't die needlessly of treatable diseases. We wanted to get rid of all the threats."

"Yes."

"The horrible thing about it is, no matter how much good you try to do, you create more ugliness at the same time."

"That must be awful."

"It is. It was better in Afghanistan, actually. In Iraq, everything was all blurred. But when I got to Afghanistan, it was clearer, believe it or not."

"I can believe it. Iraq turned into such a mess."

"Yeah. It's horrifying. There wasn't anybody in uniform who didn't want to make life better for those people. Not a one of us. But it turned out to be like opening Pandora's box.

"In Afghanistan, though, it's clearer. A lot of people just want us to go away. But a lot want us to put an end to the Taliban. I don't think they care much one way or another about Al Qaeda, but the Taliban…there's still a lot of anger against them. And every time they raid a village and destroy a girls' school, it's amazing to watch the village elders get together to rebuild it."

"Do they ask you for help?"

"Sometimes. We're still occupiers."

"It's sad."

"What?"

She tried to see his face in the dark but couldn't. "It's sad that trying to help has hurt so many."

"I know. And I don't blame the locals for having mixed feelings about us. How could I? Most of us understand how *we'd* feel if a firebase run by some other country was up the road from us."

She sighed and moved closer. "I'm sorry."

"Don't be. I volunteered. And I learned a lot."

"But now you're cut off from your mission and your buddies."

"That hits the nail on the head."

"Basically, you have to start all over."

"Yeah." He sighed. "You did it, though, didn't you?"

"Yes. But it wasn't exactly the same."

"Emotionally it's exactly the same. You gave up all your buddies in the Denver police, all your friends, and vanished into a different world to protect your daughter. The only differences between us are in degree and the idea of choice. I didn't choose to leave."

"I'm not sure I did, either." She shook her head and pressed her face into his chest. "I had no choice, not once I felt my baby was threatened."

He squeezed her. "We'll take care of her, Connie, I swear. Nothing's going to happen to her."

All of sudden she couldn't hold still. She pulled away and left the bed, throwing on her robe against the deepening chill and pacing.

"What could he want with her, Ethan? What could he possibly want with her after all this time?"

The words emerged as a cry from the abyss of fear inside her.

"I don't know," he said heavily. "I wish to God I did."

Chapter 14

They picked up Sophie from Jody's house around eight. Connie had the day off, because Gage always gave her weekends off to be with her daughter. It was one of the perks of being on a small force; personal needs could be taken into account.

Sophie looked at them sleepily from puffy eyes. Enid said the girls hadn't fallen asleep until nearly six. But when Ethan suggested they go to Maude's for breakfast, Sophie perked up. She liked steak and eggs, and didn't get them often, usually because Connie needed to watch her budget.

A crowd filled Maude's, as it usually did on Saturday mornings. Lots of folks came in from sur-

rounding ranches to take care of business in town, and
the City Diner usually topped the list of places to go.
Still, they found a booth near the back, and Sophie surprised Connie by squeezing onto the bench beside
Ethan, instead of sitting next to her.

One of those unexpected pangs hit Connie as she
wondered how much Sophie missed having a father
figure in her life. Probably a whole lot. And while Leo
could never have been a decent one, not given his violent
nature, that didn't mean Sophie didn't need a dad.

But dads didn't grow on trees. She couldn't just go out
and pluck one from a branch somewhere and bring him
home. Nor could she risk bringing home the wrong man.

There it was again, her fear of making another bad
character judgment.

Somewhere in the midst of steak, eggs and English
muffins with jam, the bomb dropped.

Sophie looked at her mother and asked, "Where's
my daddy?"

All of sudden Connie felt light-headed and faint. Her
mind seemed to have flung itself somewhere far away,
divorcing itself from her body, leaving her with tunnel
vision. Distantly, she knew that Sophie was still staring
at her, waiting.

Now she understood why Sophie had chosen to sit
beside Ethan and not her. Her heart slammed, dragging
her back to the table and out of complete shock.

"I'm not sure where your father is," she said
finally, hoping her voice sounded steadier to Sophie
than it did to her.

"Why not?"

"Because I haven't seen him in a long time."

"Why?"

So that was the way it was going to be. Connie drew a long breath. "This isn't a good place to discuss this, Sophie. Can you wait until we go home after breakfast?"

Sophie's lower lip began to tighten, then relaxed. She looked down at her plate and shrugged. "Sure."

Connie looked from her daughter to Ethan, feeling helpless, and saw sympathy in his gaze. He probably understood Sophie's side of this better than hers. God!

Her appetite gone, Connie had to force herself to eat as if nothing was wrong. Maude's ordinarily wonderful cooking tasted like sawdust and stuck in her throat.

When they got home, Sophie took Ethan's hand as they walked into the house. A message if ever there was one. Then she sat at the kitchen table and simply looked at her mother.

Ethan started the coffeepot. "Should I go to another room?"

"No," said Sophie and Connie simultaneously.

Ethan looked from one of them to the other, then shrugged and turned back to the coffeepot.

"Maybe you can help," Connie said. "You've been in Sophie's shoes."

"Only if she wants my help."

Sophie, meanwhile, had returned her attention to her mother. "Where's my daddy?"

"I told you I don't know. Why are you asking all of a sudden? You never wondered about it before."

Sophie's lower lip trembled. "Because last night at Jody's we were playing a game with her mom and dad. All my friends have dads. All of them. But not me. Why not?"

"Some of your friends' moms and dads are divorced," Connie pointed out.

"But they know them! They visit them. Is my dad dead?"

Connie, her stomach knotting until it hurt, wished she could answer with a lie. For the very first time in her life, she wanted to out-and-out lie to Sophie. "No," she said finally. "We're divorced."

"So why don't I ever get to visit him? Other kids do."

She'd already said she didn't know where Leo was. Apparently that wasn't going to suffice. She barely nodded when Ethan put a cup of coffee in front of her. His hand touched her shoulder, offering silent comfort.

"Mommy?"

Connie sighed, looking down at the table, seeking words that would satisfy without causing harm. She couldn't seem to find any.

"Your father," she said finally, "was bad to me."

"Bad how?"

"Sophie…" But the girl's stubborn expression said she wasn't going to settle for that. When and how did a seven-year-old become so mature? "Okay," Connie said carefully. "He hit me. A lot. I ran away."

Sophie frowned. "That's bad."

"Yes, it was very bad. And when I knew you were

coming, I realized I couldn't stay there anymore. I didn't want you to grow up that way."

"But why couldn't *I* see him?"

Connie stared at the child, aching, wondering how she could answer that, short of telling Sophie that her father had tried to kill her even before she was born. Sophie should never know that, should never feel that her father hadn't wanted her, had resented her presence in Connie's womb so much that he had kicked her there over and over. Only a miracle had prevented a miscarriage or damage to Sophie.

She couldn't possibly share that with her daughter. On that score, her lips had to remain sealed unto death.

Ethan sat at the table, looking from daughter to mother. "Excuse my butting in, Connie, but the truth is always best. Sophie can handle more than you think."

"But…" Even as she started to protest, Connie realized that he was right. Lies would only come between them later. But she could limit the truth for now. She *had* to.

"Okay," she said finally, looking straight at Sophie. "I ran away from him because it wasn't good for you. I went to a special home they have for women who have been hit by their husbands. A shelter."

Sophie nodded, her sleep-puffy eyes wide and attentive.

"But after they helped me get set up in a different home, a place that was supposed to be secret, he followed me home from work one day. Even though the court ordered him to stay away from me. And he hit me so hard I had to go to the hospital."

"I'm sorry, Mom." Sophie's lips were trembling.

"Is that enough, honey? Because the story is ugly."

"That's why we came here?"

"Yes. To hide even better."

"What happened to him? Did he get in trouble for hurting you?"

Connie drew a deep breath, then let it go. "He went to jail."

"For a long time?"

"Six years."

Sophie nodded. "But...do you think he would hit me, too?"

"Honey, I wish I knew. I just can't take the chance."

Sophie nodded again. Then she said, "I'm tired. I'm going to bed."

"Hug?"

Sophie came around the table and hugged her mother tight. Then, without a backward look, she disappeared up the stairs to her bedroom.

"God," Connie breathed. She put her head down on the table and battled an overwhelming urge to cry. "Did you see?" she whispered. "Did you see the look in her eyes? Like something had died."

Two powerful hands gripped her shoulders from behind, kneading gently. "She'll be okay," Ethan said reassuringly. "You'll see. Kids are resilient. But she needed to know the truth, Connie. Especially if it *is* Leo going after her."

"I know, I know." Every terrible fear that had haunted her for years seemed to be coming to fruition in this horrifying week. Fear that Leo would hurt Sophie, fear that the truth would hurt Sophie, fear that lacking a father would hurt Sophie…

And fear that she would lose Sophie. Always, always that terrible fear.

She lifted her head, unaware that tears trembled on her lower lashes. "I've been so afraid I would lose her. I've never stopped being afraid of that."

"I can tell."

"I guess, until this past week, I never faced the fact that I'd never stopped being afraid of that. Of Leo."

"Some ghosts just won't go away." He stopped kneading her shoulders and sat beside her, drawing her close, as if to protect her.

"I thought it had." She dashed the tears away. "This is ridiculous. I can't go on being a prisoner of fear. I've got to stand up to it."

"Isn't that what you're doing?"

"Not enough. Not nearly enough." She clenched her hands, then released them. "I've got to find this guy. If it's Leo, I'm going to teach him a lesson."

"Be careful what kind."

She looked at him angrily. "What do you mean?"

"Just be careful. There are lots of ways to teach a lesson, some not so good."

"I'm not an idiot!"

"But you carry a gun. Just—" He broke off, then shrugged. "Sorry. You don't need me telling you things you already know."

A shudder ripped through her. "No, you're right.

I'm not sure I'm fully rational right now. It's as if…as if a great big gaping wound has been torn open. I'm hurting so bad, and I'm so worried about Sophie. And you're right, I'm armed. If someone threatened her…"

"If someone threatens her, that's different. You know it. You're a police officer. If you need to apply reasonable force, you can and you will."

"But can I trust myself not to be *un*reasonable? Right now, I don't know. Right now, I'm afraid I might not be able to."

"Right now, you have time to think about what's going on inside you. To deal with it. You'll calm down."

"Sure. Yeah." She gave a bitter laugh. "I thought for years I was calm. Apparently I was hiding from myself, too."

"You wouldn't be the first person to do that."

"Did you see how she looked when she walked out of here, Ethan? Did you see her eyes?"

"She's tired," he said soothingly. "She's a little kid, and she's been up all night. Sure, what you told her was probably difficult to swallow, and it'll take time for her to wrap her mind around it, but most of what you saw was pure fatigue."

"How can you know that? How can you possibly know that? What if she hates me now? I sent her father to jail!"

He shook his head and caught her chin in his hand, forcing her to look at him. "Listen, Connie. Please listen. She understood that he hurt you bad enough to put you in the hospital. You underestimate her love for you if you think she's going to turn on you because Leo broke the law and went to jail."

"What if she doesn't see it that way?"

"With a mom who's a cop, I'm pretty sure she understands that. Besides, she's seven, not three. Bad people go to jail. She knows that."

"Yeah. Yeah. But other bad people aren't her dad."

His expression grew gentle. "She doesn't know the man, Connie. Her only emotional attachment to him is an attachment to an idea. He's not real. He hasn't been with her all these years. He hasn't taken care of her. Give her a chance to think about it and absorb it. She'll be okay."

"You're so sure."

"I had less reason to understand, but I did."

She couldn't deny the truth of his words. Maybe she really wasn't expecting too much of a seven-year-old. The questions had arisen, and needed to be answered. If Sophie was wondering, she deserved to know. Connie had always followed the rule that if the child asks, the child is ready to know at least something. She hadn't dumped gory details on the girl, just a general outline.

"Maybe," she said finally. "Maybe."

"Trust your daughter's love."

Surprising what a tall order that suddenly seemed to her. Yet she knew that Ethan was right. She would just have to prepare herself for an emotional reaction from Sophie. Because there was bound to be one.

There was always a price, it seemed. Even for the truth.

Chapter 15

Julia arrived home just before noon. She took one look at Connie and demanded to know what was wrong.

"Sophie asked about her father."

"Well, you knew that was coming." Julia wheeled over to the stove and poured herself a cup of coffee. Ethan rose and started to leave the kitchen, but Julia waved him back. "Stay, Ethan," she said. "You're practically part of this family now, and I suppose you were here when Sophie asked."

He nodded and resumed his chair. Julia's knowing eyes moved between them, as if she sensed the change in their relationship. But she said nothing.

"So how did she take it?"

"I don't know," Connie answered frankly. "She seemed to accept what I said, but then she went straight upstairs to bed. She was up all night, but—"

"Shh," Julia said, interrupting her. "Don't make this bigger than it needs to be. The child was probably just exhausted."

"I'm still worried," Connie told her. "How can I not be worried? And another thing, I'm wondering why this came up now. She said it was because she and the other girls played games last night with Jody's mom and dad, but that's nothing new."

Julia put her mug on the table and rearranged her chair so she was sitting comfortably facing them. "Maybe it has to do with this stranger."

Connie, thinking of last night's phone call, a call she didn't want to mention to her mother, felt a sickening jolt. "What do you mean?"

"Maybe," Julia said, "she's feeling a need for protection."

"She won't get it from that quarter," Connie said bitterly.

"She probably realizes that now," Julia agreed. "Assuming you told her something about why you had to leave him."

"I made it as sketchy as I could, but yes."

"Poor thing." Julia sighed. "For everything this mess has put *us* through this week, in her own way she's been through just as much. Maybe we haven't given enough thought to how scared she's been. Oh, I know she's acting as if it's all okay, but maybe she's trying to be strong for you, Connie. I wouldn't put it past her."

"Great." Connie closed her eyes briefly. "Here I've been assuming that she was okay, that as long as we surrounded her with protection and she knew it was there, she'd feel safe. God, I feel like a dunce."

"Well, she's not exactly acting as if she's scared of her own shadow. If she doesn't want you to know, how are you supposed to?"

"Because I'm supposed to be her mother and read between the lines. She's only seven."

"And a lot of seven-year-olds would have put that stranger behind them by now. They don't dwell on things unnecessarily, the way we adults do."

"Usually." Connie rose. "I'm going to look in on her."

She climbed the stairs with leaden feet, full of old fears and now new ones. She had honestly believed that Sophie was getting back to normal after her scare. Apparently not.

Why else all the questions about her father?

She opened the door quietly and looked in. Sophie lay in a tangle of blankets, wrapped around her favorite stuffed dog. Maybe, when this was over, she *should* let her mother get Sophie that dog. On the other hand, dogs, as wonderful as they were, meant more bills, bills that might strain an already tight budget.

She started to back out, but stopped when she heard Sophie's sleepy voice. "Mom?"

"Yes, honey?" At once she went to sit on the edge of Sophie's bed and laid a hand on her shoulder.

"It's going to be okay, right?"

"Of course it is. Are you still scared of that man?"

"Not really." Sophie rolled onto her back and looked at her. "I heard Grandma come home."

"Yes, she's in the kitchen with Ethan, having coffee."

"I like Ethan."

"So do I."

"I wish I had a dad like *him,* instead of the other kind."

Connie didn't need to ask what kind her daughter meant. "I'm sorry. I made a big mistake when I married your father."

Sophie surprised her with an impish smile. "But if you didn't marry him, you wouldn't have me."

Connie managed a little laugh. "I don't know about that. I think God always meant for me to have you. The angels saved you specially."

Sophie laughed. "I'm not that good."

"Oh, yes, you are."

Sophie's smile faded. "The man's still there."

A fist punched Connie in the chest. "Have you seen him?"

"Yeah."

"Where?"

"After school yesterday. That's why I went a different way home."

Connie didn't know what to say. For several long seconds she hung in the balance between terror and anguish. Calm, when it came, had a price. But for

Sophie's sake, she *had* to remain calm. Finally she cleared her throat. "You would have been safer staying with your friends."

Sophie shrugged. "I was safe. I'm here."

Connie didn't know how to argue with that. She didn't want to scare the child more. Yet Sophie needed to be cautious. "Honey…"

"I know. Don't trust strangers and stay with my friends." Sophie rolled over on her side again and took her mother's hand. "I'll be okay, Mommy. Don't worry."

"Just stay close, honey. Just stay close." Leaning over, Connie wrapped her daughter in a tight hug and felt those warm little arms wrap around her in return. "I love you so much."

"I love you, too, Mommy."

"Now sleep a little longer. You were up all night, Enid said."

Sophie smiled brilliantly. "It was fun."

"I bet it was. Later we'll play some games or something, okay? But get a little more sleep first."

Sophie's eyelids, still puffy with sleepiness, were already sagging to half-mast. "I really like Ethan," she said again. Then she fell sound asleep.

Connie envied her daughter's ability to drop off so quickly. These days, finding sleep herself could be a struggle. And after Sophie's little bomb, she wondered if she would ever sleep again. As if in response to an emotional overload, a kind of numbness settled over her.

She sat with Sophie for a while longer, until the little girl's breathing deepened; then, after dropping a kiss on her daughter's forehead, Connie tiptoed from the room.

Downstairs, still wearing her numbness like a cloak, she found Julia and Ethan shuffling cards. "What's going on?"

Julia grinned. "Ethan's going to teach me how to play Texas hold 'em. Don't we have chips somewhere?"

"Maybe. I seem to remember getting them for some project."

"Well, go find them, girl," Julia said. "This man wants a chance to clean me out."

Ethan's chuckle followed Connie as she went to look in the living-room credenza.

The box was still there, after all this time. She carried the chips back to the kitchen, but her mind wasn't on poker. While Ethan started divvying up the plastic chips, she said, "Sophie saw him again."

Ethan's hands froze. Julia's smile faded.

"After school yesterday. She said that's why she took a different way home."

Ethan swore softly.

Julia's face sagged. "Why didn't she tell us this yesterday?"

"I don't know." Connie, who had maintained a calm facade until this moment, couldn't hold it together any longer. Her voice stretched thin, became thready, and the panic that had been clawing at her all week grabbed her fully in its jaws.

"He's still here," she repeated. "He's still here, and Sophie saw him. How can we make her safe if he can get to her without our knowing it? How can we protect her?"

Her voice had grown shrill, and she bit back further words, knowing that she was only feeding her own panic and sense of helplessness.

But, dear God, how could she remain calm in the face of this? A stranger, maybe Leo, maybe not, was stalking her little girl. She pushed back from the table, ignoring it when the chair fell over. Like a terrified horse, she wanted to race from one end of her corral to the other and beat down the bars that held her in.

Before she could dash from the room, Ethan caught her. His strong arms surrounded her, restrained her, held her close. Surrounded her with security.

"Shh," he whispered, and stroked her hair. "Shh. She's safe upstairs right now. I swear to you, Connie, I'll be right beside her every time she leaves this house. I'll walk with her everywhere. I'll watch her when she plays. Nobody's going to hurt that child as long as I have breath in me."

Connie wanted to believe him. She desperately needed to believe him.

"It's gone past trying to keep a loose watch on her," Ethan said. "With a second encounter, we have to tighten up. Sophie may not like it, but that's the way it has to be until we catch this guy."

Connie leaned back and looked up at him. "What if it isn't Leo?" she whispered. Much as she feared Leo's violence and that it might spill over onto Sophie, there were other things to be feared more. Like real strangers. Horrible, terrible sick men who would do the un-thinkable.

Not even when she had faced an armed burglar had she felt this much gut-wrenching, sickening fear. Fear for Sophie. Fear of all the monsters that could walk into her innocent daughter's life.

A shudder ripped through her, then another. Flying apart seemed like a valid option right now. Shattering into a million pieces.

But for these few moments, Ethan's arms held her together. His strength seemed to infuse her with some-thing she desperately needed. Little by little, her shudders eased, until finally she sagged against him. He continued to hold her, seeming to understand that the strength needed to return to her muscles.

Something else began to shift within her. All of a sudden she remembered the dreams she'd had before Leo, dreams of a man who would support her and protect her and care for her, not one who would use her. Abuse her.

All those dreams had died at the end of Leo's fist, at the toe of his boot. Or so she had thought. Maybe they had only gone into hibernation.

Ethan had suddenly awakened them, but even as she realized that, she feared the cost of allowing them to reappear. Ethan wasn't here for the long haul. He'd merely come to town to meet Micah, and once he'd es-tablished whatever kind of relationship he wanted there, he would move on. Besides, he had problems of his own, and she doubted she was the solution to any of them.

There was danger here, emotional danger, but she couldn't bring herself to step away. Not yet. She needed these moments with near desperation.

Later, she thought. Later she could tear out the roots of what was trying to grow in her. Right now she needed any port in the storm. And she was sure he understood that.

When at last she regained her strength, she backed away. He let her go immediately, which she was sure was a message. No involvement, beyond protecting Sophie. Last night had been an aberration, a fulfillment of a need they both felt as solitary souls. But it had made no promises and offered no answers.

Their wounds couldn't be so easily healed, she thought, as she returned to the table. They would always be there. Healing had to come from within, and it couldn't happen if the scars kept reopening.

Julia was still sitting at the table, staring at the cards as if they could tell her the future, carefully not watching Connie and Ethan.

Then there was a knock on the side door. Connie jumped, turned and saw Micah through the glass panes. At once she leaped up to invite him in.

He was smiling, and he greeted her with a hug, Julia with a peck on the cheek and his son with a bear hug. "I thought I'd get a progress report," he said. Connie got him a cup of coffee and waved him to a chair as she resumed her seat.

"Do you have ESP?" she asked.

His face darkened. For an instant, except for Ethan's beard, father and son looked like clones of the same Cherokee ancestor.

"What happened?"

Ethan answered. "When Sophie wandered off yesterday after school? It was because she had seen the man again."

"Well, hell. I guess we need to tighten the guard."

"I'm going to be with her every minute she's out of the house and not in school."

Micah nodded. Then he looked at Connie. "How do you feel about that?"

"Better." Because if it was Leo, she didn't know how or even if she would be able to handle it.

Ethan must have noticed her glaring omission of the phone call in her recounting of events to her mother earlier, Connie thought, because he didn't mention it to Micah.

"I can't handle this," Julia said. She couldn't have been paler if every drop of blood had been sucked from her. "I'm going to my room. You'll plan better without me here gnashing my teeth and second-guessing everything because I'm a scared old woman."

Feeling a sharp pang, Connie started to rise. "Do you need help?"

"Just to get into my own bed? I think not."

The three of them listened as Julia's chair squeaked across the linoleum, then onto the wooden floor of the hall. A few moments later, her bedroom door closed.

"Okay," Micah said, leaning forward to rest his arms on the table, "what did you leave out?"

Connie looked at Ethan, wondering if he had told Micah, or if Micah just had some kind of ESP. Shaman, she thought. They both were shaman, crazy idea or not. Then she realized she would have to tell this part herself, if for no other reason than that she had been the one who answered the phone.

"I got a call last night," she said. "A man said, 'You have a beautiful daughter, Connie,' and then I hung up."

"That must have freaked you out."

"Pretty much."

The two men's faces had grown as dark and heavy as thunderclouds before a tornado.

"Your ex," Micah said.

Ethan nodded. "That's what we're thinking."

"But we can't be sure," Connie said.

"I agree it would help if we knew something certain," Micah said slowly, "but we don't. We should definitely be keeping an eye out for Leo. I'll see about getting his picture out to the deputies. But at this point, I'm not sure it would be wise to put it out to the public."

Ethan shook his head. "If it *is* Leo, we don't want to push him too hard. If he flees, it won't help us settle this matter. Besides, he's already proved violent."

"My thinking exactly." Micah looked at Connie, silently requesting her input.

"I don't think I'm a reliable judge of anything right now," she answered. "This is way too close to home. Ethan can tell you, I'm barely holding it together."

"Under the circumstances," Ethan said, "you're holding it together damn well. You won't hear any criticism from me."

"Me, neither," Micah said.

Connie smiled wanly. "I think I'll go lie down. You two can arrange everything with Gage. I'm worn out. In fact, I'm useless with worry."

"Don't stay up there if all you're doing is worrying yourself sick," Ethan said.

But that wasn't it at all. She needed to check on Sophie. She needed to be closer to her daughter. She needed some space to find at least a piece of her center to rely on. The worst way to fail Sophie right now would be by falling apart even more than she already had.

Calm. She had to find calm. Real calm. The kind of calm that would allow her to think.

Before it was too late.

Chapter 16

After the call to Gage had been made, Ethan and Micah continued to sit at the table, father and son separated by years if no longer by distance. Yet Ethan felt a recognition somewhere deep inside him, as if part of him had always known Micah. Perhaps it was just that part of him *was* Micah.

"Are you willing to stay around?" Micah asked.

"Stay around?"

"Here. In this county. You have a permanent job if you want it. Gage said so. And I'd like the time with you. Right or wrong, we've both been cheated out of something."

Ethan nodded slowly, turning inward, testing instincts and long-denied feelings. "I'd like the opportunity."

"Good. When this mess with Sophie and Connie is taken care of, Faith wants you to come stay with us for a while. She wants to get to know you, too, and she wants you to know your sisters."

Ethan nodded, feeling a small lightening in his heart. "I'd like that."

"Good." Micah drummed his fingers on the table for a moment. "I know where you've been, son. I spent twenty years doing what you did. So what happened? You're on disability?"

"IED," Ethan said succinctly. "I've got shrapnel lodged near my spine."

"Well, hell." Micah's frown deepened. "I figured it had to be bad. They aren't letting many out right now."

"No."

"So you're in danger?"

"Could be. Mostly it's just pain. But yeah, they're worried a wrong move could paralyze me."

"How are you handling that?"

Ethan shrugged. "I'm luckier than a lot of guys."

"Yeah, I know that feeling, too. Problem comes in the dead of night, when you start to think some of *them* were luckier."

A look of complete understanding passed between them.

"It gets better," Micah said. "It does. I won't say it ever completely goes away, but eventually you can look forward more than you look back."

"I hope so. Sometimes I just wish the enemy still wore uniforms."

Micah nodded. "I carry some of that with me, too."

"I'm sure you do."

Micah sighed and sipped his coffee. "I don't regret serving my country. I hope you don't."

"No. Never."

Micah nodded. "Good. You shouldn't. Some of us have to."

"I know. I'm proud that I went."

Micah reached out and clasped his son's forearm. "I'm proud of you. War creates atrocities by its very nature. But until we all learn to live in peace, some of us are going to bear that burden. I've had a lot of time to think about this, so I'll just tell you, once again, what I've learned. It's time to look to today. Today is the seed of tomorrow. And from what I can see, you're planting some mighty good seeds right now."

Ethan arched a brow.

Micah smiled faintly. "Sophie."

"Oh."

"And Connie. A man could do a lot worse than Connie."

"I don't think…"

"Not yet, maybe. But she's a good woman, through and through. Almost as good as my Faith. You'll see." He drained his mug and rose to carry it to the sink. "I'm going to get to the office, make sure that picture of Leo gets out to the force. I think we got us a snake in the corn, son, and it ain't no stranger."

Ethan watched his father leave, feeling as if an important connection had just been made. His father was no longer a stranger. He was becoming a friend.

For the first time in a long time, he smiled just because he felt like it.

In the distance he heard a rumble of thunder. Rising, he went to the front of the house to look out and see the clouds. Billowing upward, limned in white so bright it seemed to shine, and black below. Another bad one. A big one, the kind that could build up over miles of open space.

He closed his eyes as thunder rumbled again, feeling it deep inside himself. Thunder spoke, and he listened.

He had been chosen. Somehow, in some way, he had been chosen. The shaman in him rose to accept the task, whatever it might be. As thunder rumbled again, speaking in a tongue only his heart could understand, he gave thanks for the rain, for the lightning, for their cleansing, nourishing powers.

And he gave thanks that he had been brought here at this moment in time, a moment when he was needed.

Because what good was any man if he didn't serve a need?

Connie couldn't sleep. Of course, she hadn't expected to. She looked in on Sophie several times, then lay on her bed listening to the building storm. The storm, she thought, would drive Leo or whoever it was to ground. She could relax, at least for a little while.

But anxiety, her constant companion now, wouldn't let go.

She heard Ethan's footsteps on the stairs. He moved almost silently, as usual, but no matter how light his tread, he couldn't avoid all the creaky steps, even though he missed most of them.

Straining to listen, she heard him open Sophie's door, then close it. A moment later her own door opened, just as a bolt of lightning brightened the darkening afternoon. For an instant he looked as if he were stepping out of another world, a mythic being come briefly to earth. Then the lightning faded and he was Ethan again.

"You okay?" he asked.

"Can't sleep."

"Hardly surprising. Sophie's out like a light." He came into the room and lay down beside her, pulling her close with gentle hands, cradling her head on his shoulder. A shaky sigh escaped her as she relaxed against him, feeling his fingers in her hair, stroking gently.

"You know," she said presently, "I've been totally self-absorbed this week."

"You're worried about Sophie. I'm surprised you can think about anything else at all."

"But what about *you?*" she asked. "How are you doing? Are you hurting? Are you getting on with Micah? I feel so selfish."

"You're not being selfish. Micah and I are hitting it off better than I hoped. He wants me to come stay with him and Faith for a while after we take care of the threat to Sophie."

"That's a good idea." But, selfishly, she didn't think it was a good idea at all. She wanted him to stay here.

For the first time in her life she had someone she could really lean on. Someone who seemed to have shoulders broad enough to bear the burdens of life with her. And she didn't want to let him go.

Which was purely selfish. Ethan hadn't come here to take care of her. He'd come here to find a missing part of his life. Only a shrew would deny him that.

But here, right now, she had found a peace so deep that she hated the thought of losing it, even briefly. When he kissed her forehead, it felt like a blessing. From his lips, a warm relaxation spread throughout the rest of her.

He didn't say anything. It seemed as if holding her was enough for him, too.

"What about pain?" she asked. "I've seen how you move sometimes. You hurt, don't you?"

He sighed. "Most of the time," he admitted. "They say it'll get better eventually."

"How do you stand it?"

"Do I have a choice?"

"Did they give you anything for it?"

"Of course. I can have all the painkillers I want. Thing is, I don't want them."

"Why not?"

"Because I like a clear head, and because I don't want to become an addict."

"But if it gets really bad…"

"If it gets bad enough that I can't move, I might consider them. But only then. Discomfort is a state of mind to a large extent."

"Pain is a little more than discomfort."

"Same thing, different degree. A lot depends on how you look at it. It's not a fatal disease, it's an injury. Lots of people live with that."

"You're right." She sighed again and unconsciously snuggled closer. "Was it hard being raised by a single parent?"

"I suppose there were disadvantages, but none I really noticed. My mother made sure I knew her people."

"Her people?"

"Her family. Her father's side was Cherokee, which is how my uncle came to train me. Her mother's side was…" All of sudden he gave a deep chuckle. "You're not going to believe this."

"What?"

"Philadelphia mainline."

"What?" She nearly giggled. *"Mayflower?"*

"They didn't get here quite that early. But you can imagine. They weren't rich. That pretty much went away in the Great Depression, but they were still part of that crowd. And they didn't quite know what to make of me."

"Perplexing indeed."

He chuckled again. "Quite a combination. So I got exposed to two very different worlds, but mostly to her father's side. They didn't seem to care that I was half-blood."

"But the Philadelphia crowd did?"

"I don't know exactly what it was. I mean, you can see how Cherokee I look. So it wasn't as if they could ignore it. But they loved my mother, and I came with her, so they tried. Maybe they were just embarrassed that she had never married. It might have been more that than me. But my uncle…he took me to his heart. So in that sense I didn't miss out on much."

"What made you decide to go into the service?"

"That's simple. I was brought up to be patriotic, to feel that service is essential. Many Native Americans enlist for that reason. My uncle nurtured that in me, along with my more mystical side, and I guess I felt a natural urge to follow in my father's footsteps, even if I didn't know him."

"I can understand that." She hesitated. "Do you ever wonder if your mother's background and family were part of the reason she never told Micah about you?"

"Yeah, it's crossed my mind. They were a somewhat hidebound bunch. Maybe that entered into her decision. I don't know. But she never hesitated to take *me* with her when she went to visit, so I doubt she ever hid her relationship with Micah."

"Interesting."

He gave her a little squeeze. "Some questions never get answered, not in any fully meaningful way. We keep hunting for those answers, but they stay just out of reach. Thing is, I think hunting for the answers is generally more important than finding them."

"So is knowing when to stop looking," she said, thinking of Leo. "Some questions are only going to drive you crazy. Like why Leo beat me. He made me feel responsible for it. Maybe I was, in some way. But why he did it… I don't think I'll ever understand, even though I've heard all the psychobabble about it."

"Maybe he was just plain mean."

"There's that possibility, too. But you still want to ask why."

"Not necessarily. Some folks are just born with something missing."

"Also true. God knows, I saw enough of it on the streets in Denver. But the thing is, in a particular case, you never know."

"Rarely," he agreed. "But there's another thing my uncle taught me."

"What's that?"

"That no matter what we are when we're born, whether we're missing a leg or missing something else, as long as we have a working brain, we make choices. Those choices define us."

Another crack of thunder rent the afternoon, loud, as if it was right overhead. Moments later a voice called from the doorway, "Mommy, I'm scared."

Before Connie could even sit up, Sophie had catapulted herself into the bed beside her. Connie at once turned her back to Ethan and hugged her daughter. "It's loud, all right."

"It's a bad storm." Sophie snuggled in, seeming not at all fazed that Ethan was there. Seconds ticked by like heartbeats, and thunder cracked again, this time almost at exactly the same moment that lightning bleached the room.

Not long after that, Ethan wrapped his arms around both of them and pulled them close.

Throughout the storm, he sheltered them.

Chapter 17

The storm continued to rage throughout the afternoon. Around three, Connie, Ethan and Sophie went downstairs to start dinner.

"I think we should have something special tonight," Connie said.

"Yay!" Sophie clapped her hands.

"It has to be something I already have," Connie cautioned her. "I'm not going out in this storm."

Sophie immediately ran to check the refrigerator. Apparently she had something in mind, because in no time at all she'd pulled out a quart of her mother's frozen spaghetti sauce, grated parmesan and a large container of ricotta cheese, then ran to get a box of lasagna noodles from the cupboard.

"Well, that's pretty clear," Connie said, watching with a smile. "Make sure I have mozzarella."

A ball of same emerged from the cheese drawer in the fridge and joined the other ingredients on the table.

"We seem to have everything essential," Connie said.

Sophie clapped her hands again.

Connie looked at Ethan. "I hope you like lasagna."

"I love it."

Connie nodded and looked at Sophie. "So what do we do first?"

"Thaw the sauce."

"Right. You know how."

Sophie retrieved a saucepan from a lower cupboard, filled it half full with water and put in on the stove over a low flame. Then she placed the container of spaghetti sauce in it to thaw.

"Good job," Connie said. "Let's mix the filling, then put it in the fridge until we're ready to use it."

Ethan volunteered to grate the parmesan and mozzarella, saving Connie's and Sophie's knuckles. Connie and Sophie mixed the ricotta with seasonings and the mozzarella, and soon the bowl was in the fridge, covered by a plate. Then there was nothing to do but wait for the sauce to thaw.

Sophie saw the cards and chips stacked neatly on the table. "Were you going to play a game?"

Connie hesitated. "Well, it was a grown-up game."

"Oh." Sophie didn't appear at all deterred. "What kind of grown-up game?"

Connie nearly sighed. Sophie could be insistent about getting answers. "Poker," she said. "Not for kids."

"Why not, if you don't play for real money?" Sophie asked, depriving her of speech.

Connie looked at Ethan and realized he was trying not to bust a gut laughing. His face, carved as always, nevertheless seemed to be battling to remain impassive.

Julia chose that moment to roll into the room. "The girl's right," she said. "What's wrong with it, if you're just playing for worthless chips?"

"It's gambling," Connie said.

"Most things in life are," Julia retorted. "The chips are just a method of counting."

Connie didn't have an answer for that, although she tried to think up a good one. Then it struck her. "In most games you don't risk your points. You keep them."

"True," Julia agreed. "But poker has lessons of its own. Like not risking things you don't want to lose. Like making decisions and living with the outcome. Like reading other people."

Connie stared at her mother. She'd never seen this side of her before, and she wasn't sure what to make of it.

"And," Julia wound up, "there's not a thing to be lost at this table except some worthless plastic chips. In real life, when you make decisions, you have a lot more on the line."

Sophie spoke. "Don't get mad at Mommy, Grandma."

"I'm not mad at her, child." Julia smiled. "Not in the least. I just think her reaction to this game is more instinctive than valid."

Sophie's brow creased as she tried to figure that one out.

Julia looked at her daughter. "And it's the very risk that makes some things look so attractive."

Connie felt it then. An emotional blow. A comment on her marriage to Leo, maybe even on her choice of jobs. Was she drawn to risk? Had that been the factor that had gotten her into so much trouble?

Bad boy Leo. Admit it, she told herself. Admit it for once and for all. He hadn't seemed like an angel. Far from it. She'd been drawn to the bad boy and had paid dearly for the attraction. The thrill of running a risk. The stupid, stupid idea that her love would change him.

She looked down at the table without seeing it. Seeing instead her past from this new angle. And knowing, in her heart of hearts, that Julia was right. She'd been drawn to the thrill and the risk, drawn to the very challenge of possessing Leo. Then, before she really knew what was happening, she'd been ground under the heel of his boot.

All love was a gamble, of course, but some kinds of risk-taking were foolhardy. And maybe it wouldn't hurt Sophie to learn that in a game where the only risk was a few plastic chips.

She lifted her head and looked at her mother. "In that case, I think Ethan is going to teach us Texas hold 'em."

Julia smiled. "Time to learn how to gauge worth-while risks."

Ethan proved to be a patient teacher, especially with Sophie, but by the time they'd played for an hour, Sophie not only understood the relative values of the cards, but she also grasped that she needed to be careful or lose her chips.

Ethan probably folded to Sophie more than he needed to, but not so much that it was obvious. Besides, as Julia had pointed out, this game was about learning when to take risks and how much of a risk you were willing to take. Even the bluffing became a lesson, as Sophie learned she could be lied to by having large sums of chips dangled in front of her as a temptation.

By the time they stopped to make the lasagna, Sophie was beginning to understand the nuances. Connie hoped her mother was right, that Sophie could learn something about life from playing this game, even the most unsettling fact of all: that even when you did everything right, you could still lose sometimes.

Sophie enjoyed herself, regardless, and Connie found herself looking at her own life and decisions in a very different way than she had in the past. It was one thing to acknowledge that she'd chosen poorly with Leo. It was another to face up to the temptation that had sucked her in. The challenge. The risk. The notion, idiotic though it seemed to her now, that there would be a great payoff eventually.

She also noted something else, something she pondered quietly as she and Sophie layered the lasagna together: that just because you went bust on one risk, that didn't mean you couldn't take another and win. In fact, if you were ever going to win, you had to take another. The necessary element was balancing risk against the likelihood of winning.

It was something she'd never really thought about before in quite that way.

Lessons, it seemed, could sometimes be found in the unlikeliest of places.

After dinner and washing up, a general vote was held to watch *Shrek*. Sophie loved the movie, and for the first time ever, Connie watched it without feeling cynical. The ogre remained the ogre throughout, never changing. It was the princess who learned where true beauty lay.

No kissing of frogs to turn them into princes. Quite the contrary. A very different fairy tale. One that seemed strikingly apropos, all of a sudden.

Outside, the storm continued to rumble and growl, a beast at bay. She noted that sometimes Ethan would tilt his head and listen to it, as if he could hear things in that grumbling. A little shiver snaked through her as she once again had the feeling that there was something very, very special about Ethan Parish. Something beyond the ordinary.

She tried to tell herself that he was just a man like any other, that she was just being fanciful, but for some reason she couldn't shake the feeling that the man sitting on the couch on the other side of Sophie was special in some very important way. Like an old soul.

Sophie certainly liked and trusted him. In all honesty, Connie couldn't remember Sophie ever warming up this quickly to a man. But right now she was leaning against his side, and he had an arm around her shoulders, as if she belonged there.

Connie's throat tightened, and she had to blink back burning tears. She hoped nobody noticed.

But Julia did notice. Sitting in her wheelchair, inches away from Connie, she reached out and squeezed her daughter's hand. "It'll be okay," she murmured. "I promise you, Connie. It's going to be okay."

Looking at her daughter and the stranger who had come into their lives only a week ago, Connie wondered, though.

Thanks to two strangers, their lives had changed dramatically. Maybe things would be okay, but they would certainly never be the same again.

And maybe, just maybe, she wanted something more than "okay" for her life.

She caught herself, appalled by her own greediness. For now, the only thing that mattered was protecting Sophie. Only a fool would ask for more. In that snug little living room, a haven against the storm without, Connie gave thanks for the moment. *This* moment.

Sophie wanted to stay up late and watch another movie.

"We have church in the morning," Connie reminded her.

Something odd passed over Sophie's face, then fled so quickly that Connie doubted she'd seen anything.

"How come I never get to stay up late," Sophie muttered as she started up the stairs.

In that instant, blessed normalcy returned and Connie laughed with genuine ease for the first time in days.

"Cuz you're seven, kiddo," she replied.

"That's your answer to everything."

Not everything, Connie thought as she followed her daughter up the stairs. Not everything.

Life should only be so easy.

Chapter 18

The storm died sometime during the night. Connie slept restlessly, never imagining her bed could have felt so empty. But Ethan remained downstairs.

Probably having second thoughts. Every time she awoke during the night, she wished he was beside her, and every time, she reminded herself that he had plenty of reasons not to pursue matters any further. At least as many reasons as she had.

Then she would roll over and fall into a restless dream that never quite became a nightmare, but always seemed to feature something dangerous lurking just out of sight.

Finally, when the first light of dawn peeped beneath

the curtains, she climbed out of bed, dressed in warm jeans, a sweatshirt and socks, and crept as quietly as possible downstairs to the kitchen. She forced herself not to glance in the direction of the living room to see if Ethan was still sleeping.

In the kitchen, she started the coffee. It was way too early to start breakfast for the family, so she popped a slice of bread into the toaster and brought out some blueberry jam. After a night of tossing and turning, her stomach felt as if someone had filled it with acid.

Just as the coffee started to perk, Ethan appeared. He wore jeans and nothing else, causing her heart to skitter a bit at the sight of his broad, smooth chest. He was a beautiful man, she thought. She wished she could see the face behind the beard.

Then she noticed the scars. How had she missed them before? She must have been too transported when they made love to notice the multitude of white scars, some small and thin, a few larger and longer, that marked one side of his torso.

"Morning," he said. He saw where she was looking and asked, "Should I get a shirt?"

"No. No! It's just that… I guess it was really bad."

"I don't remember much of it. A blessing."

"I'm glad you're alive," she told him, meaning it as much as anything she'd ever in her life said.

"Me, too." He gave her a crooked smile. "About time I was able to say that. Sorry I fell asleep."

"It's not like you were on guard duty," she reminded him. "And you have to sleep sometimes. Besides, the house is locked, and one of us would have heard if someone tried to get in."

"Very true."

"Have a seat. I'm making toast. Would you like some?"

"Just some coffee when it's ready, thanks. I haven't been up long enough to feel hungry. You look exhausted."

She shrugged and pulled her slice of toast from the toaster. "I had a restless night. One of those where you feel like you keep waking up, but you almost never wake up enough to actually do anything about it. You know, like turn on a light and read or something. In and out like a swinging door all night."

"I'm sorry."

"It happens. In a strange way, it almost felt like when I was in the hospital." She sat at the table and began spreading jam on her toast. "When they had me drugged. I wasn't really sleeping, I had the oddest dreams, and I kept waking up but couldn't *really* wake up. Weird."

"Yeah. Been there."

She laughed quietly. "Can't blame the drugs this time. Maybe too much coffee, but not drugs."

He grinned. "Leading the clean life, eh?"

"Oh, yeah. I donate blood as often as I can, and when I go in, they have these forms. Same questions every time. I tease them that I've led a very dull life. Last time the nurse asked me if I'd ever received money for sex, I said, 'I wish.' I thought she was never going to stop laughing."

His smile broadened.

"But you know," she added more thoughtfully, "I find there are lots of questions I answer negatively that I ought to be able to answer affirmatively."

"Such as?"

"'Have you been out of the country in the last three years?' Heck, I haven't even taken a real vacation locally. So I go in and answer the questions and start thinking about taking a cruise, or visiting another country, or…"

"You'll do it someday."

She let go of her wistfulness and smiled. "Yeah, I will. Someday."

"I can't donate blood at all anymore. Been overseas too often and too much."

"That's okay. I think you've given enough, anyway."

He shook his head. "Wrong way to look at it."

"You think so?"

"You can never give enough."

As she considered his words, she nodded. "You're right. There's always a need to be met somewhere."

"Maybe I *will* have that toast," he said. When she started to rise, he waved her back. "I can make it for myself. You just rest."

"Bread's in the bread box. If you want butter…"

"I know," he smiled. "The refrigerator."

She laughed then. "Something about being a mother changes you forever. You start assuming that people need explanations for the simplest stuff."

"Looking after others is never a bad habit."

His words warmed her, and she sipped her coffee, savoring its richness, trying not to stare at the scars on his back. There were probably more she had missed, and somehow she felt embarrassed not to have noticed them. Even in the throes of their incredible lovemaking.

He popped a couple of slices of bread in the toaster, said, "Be right back," and disappeared from the kitchen. He returned before the toast was ready, wearing a sweatshirt of his own.

"Are the mornings always so chilly here?" he asked.

"Most of the year," she admitted. "At the height of summer it can get really hot in the daytime, but the nights cool down fast. I've never yet had a night when I didn't need a blanket."

"That's the best way to sleep."

They sat together for a while, sipping coffee, eating toast, no conversation necessary. They had reached that exquisite point where neither of them felt pressed to fill a silence. Connie savored that comfort. To her, that had always been a mark of a truly good relationship, when there could be companionable silence.

Eventually she glanced at the clock. "I guess we may as well go to the early service, if I can get Sophie and my mother up."

He nodded.

"Do you want to come?"

"Sure. Dress up?"

She shook her head, smiling. "Times have changed. Jeans will do."

"Nobody complains?"

"Why should they?" She shrugged. "I've often felt that God couldn't care less what we're wearing when we pray. Clothes are for other people, not for him."

"I like the way you think, Connie." Standing, he astonished her with a kiss. "I'll go wash up real quick while you wake the others."

Julia awoke quickly, with a smile, and agreed she would like to go to the early service. "Much more peaceful," she said. "Not so many folks stirring around and coughing."

Connie laughed. "Then up and at 'em. I'm going to get Sophie."

She climbed the stairs feeling better than she had in a week. Somehow Ethan's presence this morning had managed to batter back the night's vague fears, and the sunlight pouring in every window seemed to fill the world with a crisp, clean glow. The sky, she thought, would be almost unbearably clear and blue this morning.

She knocked on Sophie's door, then opened it. For an instant she didn't register what she was seeing. For an endless, eternal instant, she couldn't put the pieces together.

"Sophie?"

No answer.

"Sophie?" She turned from the bedroom and ran to the hall bathroom, finding it empty.

Then she screamed. *"Sophie!"*

Only silence answered her.

Chapter 19

Five sheriff's cars filled the tree-lined street. Gage and Micah were there, along with her other friends. Other cars were already out on the streets and ranging the countryside, searching. Every one of them had Leo's arrest photo.

Connie had pulled on her own uniform and gun, ready to get going. But Gage wouldn't let her, not just yet.

"The doors were locked," she kept saying.

Gage looked at Ethan. "You'd have heard her."

"If she'd come downstairs, yes," he said. "I know myself well enough that even when I sleep, I'm still alert if I need to be. And those stairs creak."

"So that leaves…" Gage's scarred face frowned at the dormer of Sophie's room.

"Exactly," Ethan said. "It wouldn't have been hard for her to get down."

"Or someone to get in," Connie said.

Ethan shook his head. "A normal-size man would have made too much noise. This room's right over the living room."

She turned on him. "Are you saying Sophie left on her own?"

He didn't answer, but his dark eyes said everything.

"Why would she do that, Ethan? *Why?*"

"She said she saw him on Friday. Maybe she talked to him. If it's Leo…"

Connie bit her lip. "You think he could have talked her into meeting him?"

"Remember her questions?"

Connie nodded slowly. It was all starting to make sense, and she hated the sense it was making. She looked from Gage to Ethan. Her voice came out as little more than a terrified whisper. "He won't hurt her. Will he?"

Nobody could truthfully answer.

"Why the hell couldn't he just knock on the door like an ordinary person?" she demanded.

Gage pulled no punches. "I know you're upset, Connie. Hell, I'm upset, too. But if he'd knocked on the door, would you have let him meet Sophie?"

Despair swamped her. "No."

"That's probably why, then."

"But what if he takes her away? What if he kidnapped her?"

That was the ugly possibility. The one they all feared.

"We're working on it," Gage assured her. "I'm assuming she didn't leave until the storm let up, so she's only got a few hours lead on us. Everyone's looking, Connie, and I've notified the neighboring counties. He won't get past us."

Given the wide-open spaces that made up so much of this part of the state, Connie had her doubts. Doubts she didn't want to think about right now.

"Okay," Gage said. "We're all fanning out. Julia, you stay here to wait for Sophie. She might just come skipping home. Micah, see that Julia has a radio, so she can call us directly."

Micah nodded and went to get a spare from his car.

Gage turned to Ethan and Connie. "You two stay together. I know I can't keep you from looking, Connie. But don't do something you'll live to regret. Something Sophie will live to regret."

She knew exactly what he meant, because right now, in the midst of her terror, she could have killed Leo without a second thought.

"She won't," Ethan said, speaking for her. Taking responsibility for her. "She won't."

Gage clasped Connie's shoulder. "Word's getting out, Connie. At the church, at Maude's. Everyone in town is going to be looking very soon."

She nodded, trying to take heart from that, but she

couldn't. What if someone angered Leo or scared him into doing something awful? But she knew as well as anyone that when this county went on alert, there was no way anyone could keep her neighbors from taking a hand. That was the way they'd always lived. Today they would beat the bushes, and if they found any kind of information about where Sophie had gone, they would gather and form a search party faster than you could say lickety-split.

Cars began to peel away as directions were given, but Connie and Ethan remained. He kept looking at the dormer and the cottonwood that nearly brushed the roof.

Connie spoke. "You think she climbed down that tree."

"That or one of the others. Weird, but the first time I walked around the house, I saw those trees as a security risk. I had to remind myself I wasn't in Afghanistan."

"You'd have cut them down?"

"Back there, yeah."

She nodded, trying to focus on the problem in the now, not on her fears. Fear could only inhibit clear thinking, and she needed her mind as clear as it had ever been.

Okay, she told herself. It was probably Leo. The only reason she could think of for him to develop this interest in Sophie was to get at her. The terrifying question, of course, was what kind of punishment did he want to inflict on her?

But another possibility existed, a slim one. Maybe during his years in prison he'd learned something. Maybe…

No, she couldn't allow herself to think he might be a changed man. Without proof, that could only be a vain hope.

Ethan started toward the side of the house, to the tree nearest the dormer. Connie's heart rose to her throat at the thought of Sophie crawling across the wet roof to grab on to that tree and climb down. Had her daughter lost her mind?

No, of course she hadn't. Sophie wanted something she felt her mother had denied her. Talk about a knife in the heart.

Near the base of the tree, Ethan paused and pointed. "There? You see?"

She did indeed see. Someone had walked on the wet grass, although with all the rain they'd had, the grass had bent, not broken.

"Small footprints."

Connie nodded. It was then that Micah joined them. "Julia has a radio," he said. "Am I seeing what I think?"

Ethan looked at him. "I think she went toward the park."

"That general direction." Father and son locked eyes. Micah spoke. "I'll follow in the car."

Ethan nodded. "Connie, why don't you ride with Micah?"

"Ethan…"

"I can track better if I'm not disturbed."

Feeling almost as if she'd been slapped, she finally gave a short nod and went to join Micah in the car.

"It's nothing personal," Micah said to her as he began to ease down the street behind Ethan. "A tracker can't afford to be disturbed."

"I get it." But her voice came out tight from her huge number of warring emotions. The only things she *didn't* feel right now were happiness and peace. All the rest of it was there, though. All the ugly, terrifying emotions people associated with their less civilized parts.

Ethan was walking along the sidewalk now, looking from side to side, apparently trying to see if footprints left the pavement at any point.

Finally they reached the park, and Ethan squatted.

"What's he doing?" Connie asked.

"The rain we had is actually a help for this. When he gets down like that, he can see anywhere there's been a disturbance in the moisture pattern."

"But it could be anybody."

"At this hour on a Sunday morning, it's not likely to be."

She couldn't argue with that. Why should she? Besides, what other method did they honestly have, other than a wide search net?

"If anything happens to her…" Connie didn't finish the thought. She couldn't. Her hands clenched into fists so tight that her short nails bit into her palms. "Micah…"

"I know." His tone was grim. "I know. I killed once

to protect Faith from her ex. I've got kids of my own. Trust me, Connie, you won't get to your gun fast enough."

She believed him. One look at his face, and she believed him.

And there was Ethan, moving now along the edge of the park. His face looked every bit as grim and determined as his father's. In her heart, she understood that these two men were as dedicated to finding Sophie safe and alive as she was. Gage, too, she thought, remembering his face. He'd lost his whole family to a car bomb many years ago. He knew what she was facing.

The support from those three was enough to light a flame of courage in her heart. They would get Sophie back. Soon.

Back at the sheriff's office, a command post was building. Velma ran off copies of Leo's photo and handed them out to the locals. Pretty soon every road in the county had a patrol on it, even the muddiest back roads, where ranchers and their hired hands patrolled with shotguns, looking behind every bush and tree. In town, residents combed every street, alleyway and backyard. With cell phones and CBs, contact was maintained. Airwaves crackled with calls as people reported nothing on one road and announced their intention to move to another. Others mounted their horses to go places vehicles couldn't on the muddy ground.

Micah and Connie heard a great deal over the car's

radio. "That bastard is gonna need a hole in the ground," Micah remarked.

They were now following Ethan down a quiet side street. He strode now, as if he knew exactly where he was going. Micah picked up the radio. "What's going on, Ethan?"

"She was picked up by a car at the park. I can just about see the tire tracks heading this way."

Micah looked at Connie. "He's good. Trust him."

"He's all I can trust," Connie said.

"I meant something else, but I guess now's not the time. You can trust all your neighbors, Connie. That's one thing I've learned living here. When the chips are down, these folks get together."

"I know. God, I wonder…" She trailed off.

"Wonder what?"

"Oh, last night we played some poker. Julia thought it would be a good lesson for Sophie in risk-taking and calculating risks versus benefits."

"And you're wondering if that had something to do with Sophie's decision to climb out her window."

"Yes. What if I helped her to take this risk?"

Micah fell silent for a bit as they followed Ethan. They were getting closer and closer to one of the least-used county roads, one that had no destination other than the mountains. Then he spoke. "You can't blame yourself. I doubt she made up her mind based on a poker game."

"She's seven. Anything could have been enough to influence her."

"Exactly. That's the point, Connie. She's *seven.* She must have been thinking about doing this since Friday, when she saw him. It was probably planned then. I don't think a card game had anything to do with it, any more than playing Candyland would have. Regardless of what your mother might have said, Sophie's very young. I doubt she was extrapolating the lessons of poker to life."

"Except for what my mother said."

"Julia was talking over Sophie's head. Maybe in time she could have learned something valuable from the game, but from playing for an hour or two? Too abstract."

"I hope you're right."

"I've been raising my own. At that age, they're pretty damn literal."

She nodded, shoving down another wave of guilt and fear that she had somehow pushed Sophie into this craziness.

She should have tried to establish a relationship between Sophie and Leo, she thought now. Maybe if her daughter had seen him in prison often enough, she wouldn't now have the kind of curiosity and need that made her want to climb out a second-story window.

If it *was* Leo.

That thought terrified her. A total stranger scared her more than Leo. At least he was a known quantity. His violence, ugly as it was, hadn't been directed at children in some sick way. So why would he want to kill Sophie? To punish Connie? Somehow that didn't add up in her mind.

The problem was, nothing was adding up quite right. Fear and terror rode her shoulders, whispered in her ears and interfered with rational thinking.

They reached the county road. Ethan squatted, looking both ways, then came back to the car. He climbed in the back seat.

"Drive slow," he said. "They headed west. What's out there?"

"Nothing," Micah said. "Mountains. He could have come back into town."

"Drive up to the western edge, then I'll check for turnoffs."

Connie felt an absolute wave of certainty come over her. "He didn't come back into town. He had to know everyone would be looking for him. He took her to the old mining camp."

For several moments the car was filled with a silence interrupted only by the quiet hum of the engine and the whine of tires on wet pavement.

All of sudden Micah floored it. "You're right," he said grimly. "And that place is probably as dangerous as he is. Maybe more so."

Connie nodded, feeling the blood drain from her face. Unstable ground, old shafts ready to cave in, buildings standing merely from the pressure of memory. Even without Leo, Sophie could get killed up there just by taking one wrong step. And Connie doubted Leo had any idea just how dangerous the place was.

"Hurry," she said. "Oh, God, hurry!"

Chapter 20

The closer they drew to the mountains, the worse the road grew. Past the last ranch, it was mainly used in the autumn by hunters, and sometimes in summer by people who wanted to hike. After the winter, it desperately needed grading again, but as muddy and rutted as it was, good drainage kept them from bogging down. Better still, they could see the fresh tire tracks made since the night's rain.

Micah spared no speed, sometimes skidding in the mud, but going as fast as he possibly could.

As they began the climb, trees closed in around them.

"I've gotta slow down, Connie. We can't risk driving past him."

"I know. I understand." And she did. But she hated it. She peered intently into the shadows beneath the evergreens, feeling the air grow steadily cooler as they climbed. Ethan gripped her shoulder and squeezed comfortingly.

"I'm looking out the left side," he said. "You concentrate on the right."

"Thanks."

Finally they rounded the last curve before the old mining camp, and Connie gasped as she saw the vehicle, a battered old pickup, muddy and almost colorless, parked near the warning sign that advised would-be explorers of the many dangers.

She wanted to jump out before Micah had fully stopped their SUV, but Ethan held her back, his fingers tightening. "Just wait," he said. "You don't want to break a leg."

"How could he take her in there, with all those signs?"

Nobody had an answer for that. Nor did anybody want to say that Sophie might not even be there.

"We'll split up and circle," Ethan said. "Around the outside. Maybe he didn't take her in there, but if we circle, we'll hear or see something if he did. And if he didn't, they can't be far away."

"He had to have heard our car coming," Connie said. Her heart beat a rapid tattoo, and she began to breathe heavily.

"I know," Ethan said. "So we've got to approach carefully."

"I'm no good at tracking," Connie said. "You two do the perimeter. I'm going in there."

The two men hesitated, but finally nodded. "All right," Micah said.

"I'll disable his vehicle," Ethan added. He slipped out of the car and within a minute had removed the distributor cap from beneath the truck's hood. He shoved it into a pocket.

Then, speaking not a word, he and Micah signed to each other and headed out in opposite directions. Connie stood at the sign, looking into the camp, her mind trying to chart the most dangerous places. Once, this had been a small town, but now collapsing cabins and mine shafts could be found all over the mountainside. Most of the shaft openings had been boarded over, many marked with the radiation-hazard trefoil. Radon gas built up in the shafts, and some shafts had exposed uranium deposits.

And the ass had brought her daughter *here*.

Anger resurged, more helpful than the fear that had dogged her. Unsnapping her holster guard, she walked into the camp.

The rains had made the place even more treacherous. Running in rivers, pooling in potholes, undoubtedly pouring down shafts. Eroding support everywhere. The old miners had been good builders, but not even they could prevent the ravages of time. Timber rotted. Water carried away supporting ground and rock.

Almost all the tailing mounds had been carted away years ago by the Environment Protection Agency. The stuff the miners didn't want contained all kinds of toxic elements that the rain swept into rivers. Even today, where tailings remained, nothing grew.

The work done here had created a scar on the land-scape that not even more than a century had repaired. Trees had not returned, and even scrub still didn't grow in most places.

She walked cautiously, pausing often to listen and look around. If there were any cracks in the ground to give her warning, the rain had filled them in, making this place more dangerous than ever. She tried to remember from times past where the firmest ground lay, but it had been so long…

Then she heard it. *Sophie's voice.*

She turned immediately to the left, looking. She couldn't see a damn thing other than tumbled buildings and rusting equipment. She bit back an urge to call her daughter's name, for fear she might precipitate some-thing.

Then she heard it again. A child's piping voice, speaking quietly, but sounding normal. Not sounding hurt or frightened.

Thank God!

Trying not to let eagerness overwhelm caution, she moved as lightly and quickly as she could, listening intently and scanning the ground for dangers.

To the left again. Along what had once been a narrow street lined by small dwellings. Rotting, sagging, windows gaping without glass or other cov-erings except for a faded scrap that might once have been a curtain. Boarded-up doors to discourage explorers. More warning signs, posted in just the past couple of years after a hiker was injured by a collapsing building.

Then, oh, God, then…

Sophie's voice again, coming from just behind one of the buildings. Quiet. As if she was trying not to be heard. Then another voice, this one even quieter, low, a man's voice.

Pulling her gun, Connie held it in both hands and slowly worked her way around the weatherbeaten remains of some long-dead person's dreams.

Her heart stopped, and she rounded the back corner. There was Sophie, clad in jeans, sweatshirt and a pink raincoat, sitting on a camp stool. On the muddy ground in front of her sat a man. Connie could see only his back, covered by a denim jacket. His hair was long, graying. She didn't recognize him at all.

Slowly raising her gun, she pointed it straight at the man's back.

"Sophie," she said, keeping her voice calm, "move away from him."

"But, Mommy, it's Daddy."

The man turned his head, and with a slam, Connie recognized him. Leo, aged by his time in prison, looking seedy and too thin.

"Sophie," she said, keeping her gun leveled. "Come here. Now."

"Mommy, don't shoot him."

"I won't shoot him if you come here."

Scowling, Sophie slid off the camp stool and walked toward her mother. Connie, tensed in expectation that Leo might reach for Sophie to use her as a hostage, was relieved when he let their daughter pass him without even twitching a muscle.

As soon as Sophie reached her side, Connie wrapped one arm around her, gun still pointed at Leo.

"You kidnapped her," she said.

"No. She came to me."

"I did, Mommy."

"The minute you put her in the car with you, you kidnapped her." She keyed her shoulder mike. "Micah? Ethan? I've got her. Leo's here. I'm behind a building one block from the town center, uphill."

They rogered her simultaneously over the crackling radios.

"Don't you read the signs, Leo? You could have gotten her killed!"

"I checked the place out. I've been here a while."

"Why? *Why?*"

"Can I get up?"

"You just stay where you are." No way was she going to let him move until she had backup.

He sighed and shook his head. "I was a bastard, Connie. I've had plenty of time to face that fact."

"Yeah, rehabilitated by prison. Next you'll be thumping the Bible at me."

To her amazement, his face actually saddened. "Yeah," he said quietly. "I found God. About time."

She hesitated, holding Sophie even tighter. "I'm

supposed to believe that—when you kidnapped my daughter?"

"She's *my* daughter, too! I figured that one out, finally."

"You never cared before."

"I never did a lot of things before that I should have. Instead, I did a lot of things I *shouldn't* have. I had this cell mate in prison. He was in for dealing. He spent the whole damn time whining about how much he missed his kids. At first it pissed me off. But then I began to realize something."

"Yeah?"

"Yeah. I realized I'd thrown away the only good things in my life. The only things that mattered."

"Amazing conversion."

He shook his head. "I don't expect you to believe me. But I'd never hurt a hair on Sophie's head."

"Then why the hell didn't you just knock on my door, instead of putting her and me through hell for a week?"

"Because I knew you'd never let me see her. I tried to talk to you on the phone, but you hung up before I could say anything more than that you have a beautiful daughter."

That was true. The truth of it pierced her. But not enough to make her trust this man.

Ethan appeared, his own gun unholstered, and took up position to one side. "Sophie, are you okay?"

"I'm fine," the girl said. "Why is everyone pointing guns at my daddy?"

Connie answered. "Because he did a bad thing when he brought you up here."

"No, he didn't. I wanted to talk to him. He's my daddy!"

Slowly, without permission, Leo rose and put his hands in the air. "So send me back to prison," he said. "It doesn't matter. I got to see her. And I'll be gone in a couple of months, anyway."

Connie's hand wavered, and she lowered her pistol. "What kind of crap is that?"

"No crap," Leo said. "You can check. Remember how you always said I should quit smoking? You were right. I got lung cancer. Nothing they can do."

That explained why he looked so worn and way too thin. And now, as she stared at him, she could see lines of pain around his eyes and mouth.

Micah had appeared to one side, and now he spoke. "This isn't a good place to talk. Let's go back into town, where it's safe and dry. We can sort it out there."

Connie slipped her pistol back into its holster and snapped the guard strap into place, then turned to squat and hug Sophie as tightly as she could. "Do you know how scared I was? Do you have any idea?"

"I'm sorry."

"Next time, talk to me first. *Please.*"

Sophie nodded, but she was watching Micah and Ethan walk her father away. "You won't put him in jail, will you?"

Connie hesitated, but as she looked into her daughter's eyes, she realized there could be a worse crime than the scare she'd had this morning. The seeds of it were already in her daughter's clear blue eyes.

"Not if he's been telling the truth. Fair enough?"

That seemed to satisfy Sophie, for now at least. Taking her mother's hand, she followed her back to the SUV.

Chapter 21

Connie sat on the edge of Sophie's bed, holding her hand. She'd never felt so tired in her life, but the strain was mostly gone. The threat to her daughter had been eliminated. All the adrenaline that had been keeping her going seeped away like gas from a punctured balloon.

"I know he was bad to you," Sophie said. "But he was nice to me."

"And I promised you could see him here, in this house, if his story checks out."

"I know. People can get better, Mommy."

Connie had her doubts, but she wasn't about to share them with Sophie. People *could* change, she supposed.

After all, that was the basis of her religion. The fact that it didn't often happen didn't mean it never could.

The thought of Leo dying… Well, despite everything, that disturbed her. Saddened her. She didn't have a lot of feelings about him one way or another anymore, but she could still be saddened by the news. As she would be for anyone.

She only cared that he treated Sophie well. It would have been kinder if he'd stayed away, so Sophie wouldn't have to suffer through his death, but that had become moot. In the meantime, she could only hope that Sophie garnered some good memories to make up for not having a father all this time.

"Where's Ethan?" Sophie asked.

"Downstairs, I think."

"I want a good-night hug."

"I'll call him." She wished she knew if this growing attachment was a good thing. Ethan had proved himself to be a good and caring man, but if he moved on, and he most likely would, Sophie would suffer another loss. But she could no longer prevent that. Too late. Amazing how much had suddenly become too late, even as the pressure of the threat lifted.

But life brought loss to everyone sooner or later. She couldn't shield Sophie from everything forever. She'd learned that the hard way this week.

Ethan came up in answer to her call and bent over the bed to give Sophie a warm hug. "No more shinnying out the window, Missie, or I'll handcuff you to your bed at night."

Sophie giggled, the happiest she'd sounded all day. "I won't, I promise."

"Sleep tight," he said, and dropped a kiss on her forehead.

Connie waited with Sophie until she slipped into sleep. Then, feeling as if she could barely lift her legs, she went to her own room. She stopped just inside the doorway, surprised to see Ethan there, standing by the window, looking out.

She hesitated on the threshold, then entered and closed the door. "I suppose you'll be moving in with Faith and Micah soon." And then moving even farther away. Her heart plummeted at the thought.

He turned from the window to face her. "Actually," he said slowly, "I was hoping you would let me stay here."

"Here? On the couch?"

He took a step toward her. "No. Here. With you."

She caught her breath, feeling her fatigue drain away. A flicker of wild hope ignited. "Ethan?"

He seemed to glow with some inner strength and fire before her very eyes. His very presence pulled her, as if by magical force.

"I wasn't looking for this," he said. "I never expected to find it, frankly. I was just going to pass through, get a few questions answered and drift on until I found…something. I had no idea what it would be."

"But?"

"But here it is. Right here. With you and Sophie. I

was on a quest, and it ended right here. If I have to leave you, I won't go farther than Micah's place. And I'll keep beating on your door and bringing you roses until you say yes. Because I love you, and I want to spend the rest of my life with you."

For an instant Connie doubted her own ears. Then her whole body lightened as she realized she had finally let go of her own self-doubts and wariness, at least with this man. Then, as if carried on angel wings, she flew across the room to land in Ethan's strong arms.

"I don't want you to go. I never want you to go!"

He laughed and lifted her right off her feet. "I take it that's a yes?"

"Yes, yes, yes, and I love you, too!"

He smiled down at her, his face warmer than she had ever seen it. "Will you marry me?"

She pressed her face to his shoulder, overwhelmed by joyful tears. Her prayers had been answered, including one she had barely acknowledged. Sophie was safe, and Ethan wanted her. Her heart swelled until she ached with gratitude. "Yes, Ethan. Oh, yes!"

"Do you think Sophie will be okay with it?"

"Let's go ask her right now."

A minute later the quiet house was filled with a little girl's voice crying, "All *right!*"

The stranger had brought peace, and it settled gently over the house as happy voices talked well into the night.

Even bad things could bring some good, Connie thought much later, as she lay in Ethan's arms, snug and safe.

And this was as good as it could get.

* * * * *

REQUEST YOUR FREE BOOKS!

2 FREE NOVELS PLUS 2 FREE GIFTS!

Silhouette® Romantic

SUSPENSE

Sparked by Danger, Fueled by Passion!

YES! Please send me 2 FREE Silhouette® Romantic Suspense novels and my 2 FREE gifts (gifts are worth about $10). After receiving them, if I don't wish to receive any more books, I can return the shipping statement marked "cancel." If I don't cancel, I will receive 4 brand-new novels every month and be billed just $4.24 per book in the U.S. or $4.99 per book in Canada, plus 25¢ shipping and handling per book plus applicable taxes, if any*. That's a savings of at least 15% off the cover price! I understand that accepting the 2 free books and gifts places me under no obligation to buy anything. I can always return a shipment and cancel at any time. Even if I never buy another book from Silhouette, the two free books and gifts are mine to keep forever.   240 SDN EEX6   340 SDN EEYJ

Name   (PLEASE PRINT)

Address   Apt. #

City   State/Prov.   Zip/Postal Code

Signature (if under 18, a parent or guardian must sign)

Mail to the Silhouette Reader Service:

IN U.S.A.: P.O. Box 1867, Buffalo, NY 14240-1867
IN CANADA: P.O. Box 609, Fort Erie, Ontario L2A 5X3

Not valid to current subscribers of Silhouette Romantic Suspense books.

Want to try two free books from another line?
Call 1-800-873-8635 or visit www.morefreebooks.com.

* Terms and prices subject to change without notice. N.Y. residents add applicable sales tax. Canadian residents will be charged applicable provincial taxes and GST. Offer not valid in Quebec. This offer is limited to one order per household. All orders subject to approval. Credit or debit balances in a customer's account(s) may be offset by any other outstanding balance owed by or to the customer. Please allow 4 to 6 weeks for delivery. Offer available while quantities last.

Your Privacy: Silhouette is committed to protecting your privacy. Our Privacy Policy is available online at www.eHarlequin.com or upon request from the Reader Service. From time to time we make our lists of customers available to reputable third parties who may have a product or service of interest to you. If you would prefer we not share your name and address, please check here. ☐

SRS08

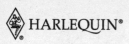

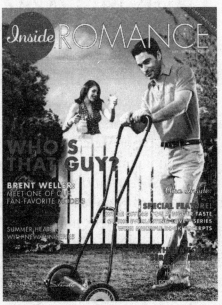

Silhouette®
Romantic
SUSPENSE

COMING NEXT MONTH

#1523 DAREDEVIL'S RUN—Kathleen Creighton
The Taken
After Matt Pearson suffered a tragic rock-climbing accident that left him wheelchair-bound, he left his fiancée and business partner, Alex Penny. Years later, Matt's long-lost brother is determined to reunite Matt and Alex. But their planned trip back to the mountain reveals an enemy bent on destroying them.

#1524 KILLER AFFAIR—Cindy Dees
Seduction Summer
Can-do girl Madeline Crummby is off to a remote Fijian island to review an exclusive resort, and she hires Tom Laruso, a burned-out bodyguard, to fly her there in spite of an approaching hurricane. When their plane crashes, they are trapped on an island…with a serial killer.

#1525 HER BEST FRIEND'S HUSBAND—Justine Davis
Redstone, Incorporated
Gabriel Taggert's wife, Hope, disappeared eight years ago. Now her best friend, Cara Thorpe, has received a postcard from her, mailed on the day she vanished. Gabriel and Cara set off to find out what happened to Hope, and along the way they discover their true feelings for each other.

#1526 THE SECRET SOLDIER—Jennifer Morey
All McQueen's Men
When Sabine O'Clery is kidnapped in Afghanistan, Cullen McQueen is the perfect candidate to rescue her. Having reached a remote Greek island vulnerable Sabine reaches out to Cullen, and their farewell kiss is captured by the press. With her kidnappers still after her, Cullen must save Sabine again, risking his life…and his heart.